Sigmund the Red, a young V
his sea wolves southwards. (
they must protect the pricel
spent years creating. Diarmu:
in charge of the golden book.   ....., ..icy must
risk the dangers of Corrievrechan whirlpool ...

Sea Wolves
from the North

By the same author
Magus the Lollipop Man (Canongate 1981)
Kelly: a novel (Wolfhound, 1981)

For Maureen

SEA WOLVES
from the North

Michael Mullen
Illustrated by Jeanette Dunne

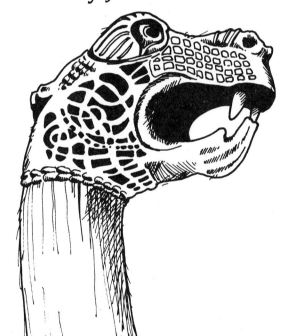

WOLFHOUND PRESS Dublin

CANONGATE Edinburgh

Published by
WOLFHOUND PRESS, 68 Mountjoy Square, Dublin
and co-published in England, Scotland and Wales by
CANONGATE PUBLISHING LTD., 17 Jeffrey St., Edinburgh.

British Library Cataloguing in Publication Data
Mullen, Michael
    Sea Wolves from the north
    I. Title
    823'. 914 [J] PZ 7

    ISBN 0-905473-94-9 Wolfhound Press
    ISBN 0-86241-038-X Canongate

Published with the assistance of the Arts Council
(An Chomhairle Ealaíon), Dublin, Ireland.
Cover design by Jarlath Hayes.
Cover illustration, Jeanette Dunne.
Typesetting by Leaders, Swords.
Printed and bound in the Republic of Ireland.

Contents

CHAPTER 1

The Longship

THE VIKING, SIGMUND THE RED, set out from the south of Norway in early summer. During the winter, in a deep fjord and protected from storms, carpenters under thatched sheds had finished the vessel. It was long, shallow and fair, no plank thicker than an inch. From tail–stern to dragon–head, it was slim of line, a sleek sea-monster which would carry its crew down along the coast to prey on the villages and monasteries of Scotland. The beams and planks had staggered joints so that the ship was as supple and pliable as hide.

For many years the oak timbers had seasoned in the forest. Then the best carpenters of the villages had been gathered to build the ship. They worked from a large model kept in the hut of Sigmund the Red. They knew the nature and the humours of the sea. They had placed the oar ports three planks down from the rail, so that the oars would not enter the water too steeply. With shields strapped above these oar ports they would be protected both from the sea and any enemy that might attack them. The shields were bright scales on a sea-serpent's body.

The women in the village had stitched the lengths of woollen cloths together into a large sail, strong enough to bear the strains of wind and storm. Upon this open space of canvas, Sigmund would place the emblem of the sea-serpent.

He had planned this ship for a long time. At sixteen he had sailed under Ulick the Fair. Even then he was a man of great strength. His red beard, his red hair and his sudden angers were known along the fjord. Five years he had sailed under Ulick the Fair, issuing each year from the narrow fjords when spring came and the ice melted. Ulick had trained him to sail by sea signs. He could smell his position on the sea when others thought themselves to be lost. His eyes followed the flight of the migrating birds. The skua gulls and the solan geese plotted his course and a handful of sea weed, dredged out of the sea, confirmed his position.

Ulick the Fair had been a sheep stealer but not so his second captain, Knut of the Sword. He had penetrated further down the coast of Scotland and maintained strict control over his crews. He attacked only the monasteries and the rich villages. The world of the south was soft and rich.

Now, after all his years sailing under many sea captains, he possessed his own ship. During the winter he had gathered his crew. They were all tested men. They accepted his offer. Half the booty went to the ship and the captain, the rest was divided among the crew members.

The ship was ready in late spring. They launched it into the fjord. It floated like a proud swan. It was firm and well balanced and could carry a crew of forty. Standing upon the prow of the ship he chanted a pagan prayer.

'Odin and Thor, Gods of the north, see us safely on our journey. Send the lesser gods to fight on our side. Fill our hold with booty and send fair winds to fill our sails. May our swords be red with the blood of our enemies and our spoils rich beyond reckoning.'

A week later the ship was provisioned and ready to sail. Sigmund the Red had fitted on his leather jerkin, studded with disks of iron to protect him in battle. He stood out above the other crew members as they made their way down to the timber pier. His shoulders were strong and broad, and his red hair fell down brightly on them. By his side hung his sword, silver-handled. He stood for a moment and looked at the ship. It was perhaps the finest ship ever built in the fjords and had sinews of a spirited animal.

'And what do you think of my ship?' Sigmund the Red asked an old sea pirate who had come down to the pier.

'Truly Sigmund, she is a ship above all ships. She is light in the water and turns well to the side rudder and the oar. She seems to have been born for the sea. She is almost a sea creature. Some ships are built without life but not this ship. If I had all my years back again and spirit in my blood and supple oar muscles I would sail under you, Sigmund.'

Sigmund the Red looked at the old man, now stooped, but who once had stood at the prow of his own vessel and directed her down through the fjord. His knarled hand held a staff to support him. But his eyes brightened when he looked at the ship. The sea urge was still in his heart.

'I have something for you, Sigmund,' he said. With shaking hand, he opened his stained leather satchel and took out several squares of supple calf hide, stitched at the back into a rough manuscript. 'These are markings I made many years ago of the coast to the south. I drew the mountain shapes and marked the villages. You will not have to come inshore to the land and your attacks can be attacks of surprise.'

'What can I give a man in return for such treasures?' Sigmund asked.

'Bring me back two barrels of wine from the south. You will find them in the monasteries with the other treasures.'

'You shall have your barrels of wine.'

'And do not forget, Sigmund, to offer the gods the cup of blood before you sail. Never forget the offering to the sea and the sky. Bad fortune will attend you, Sigmund, if you do not follow the old ways.'

'I will follow the old rites. Come with me to the place of sacrifice.'

They left the pier and the old man hobbled along beside him down the path to the stony beach. The villagers were waiting for Sigmund. Now they gathered about in a circle. Sigmund walked to the rough stake where the sheep had been tethered. With a quick movement he drew his dagger and cut its throat. As the blood splurted out he gathered it in a broad earthen dish. Raising the vessel shoulder high he looked towards the blue sky.

'Thor, God of Thunder,' he called, 'You who dwell in Asgard, hear the voice of Sigmund the Red. We have heard the thunder of your chariot wheels crossing the heavens. We have seen your lightning root itself in the mountains. Be on our side in battle and let your voice fill our enemies with terror.'

His loud voice carried out over the waters of the fjord and echoed off the mountain face until it filled the valley with many voices. He finished the prayer and poured blood into the water. The winding stain was carried towards the sea. He then sprinkled the ship with blood and gave the empty vessel to a youth to carry back to the rude temple. It was now time to weigh anchor.

His men took their positions in the ship. He had chosen them for their knowledge of the sea, their ferocity in battle. Some of them would have to be watched. They often drank too much and became quarrelsome. Some might become mutinous. Many ships had returned without their sea captains.

His men placed their oars in the oar ports. He beat the drum. They raised their oars out of the water. Then he began the slow drum beat. The fine oars cut smartly into the water and the ship began to move out towards the centre of the fjord. They swung the ship about. It was taken by the current. They hoisted the square sail carrying the green and red figure of the serpent. It held the wind evenly and the ship moved under sail.

Sigmund the Red, standing at the prow of his ship, looked shorewards. The village was cramped under the hills of pine. He could see the small pockets of land where they grew rye in the summer. People were running down the stony beach waving to him. The ship moved down stream, passed a steep cliff and the village was out of sight.

All his life Sigmund the Red had waited for this day. He looked at the sky, empty of cloud. The sun was catching the upper peaks of the mountains which carried perpetual caps of snow and was turning them to gold. The snow would be melting among the pines, feeding the cascades which fell over the cliffs in strands of foam and mist.

By now the sun had marched halfway across the heavens. At the third quarter of the day they would enter the open sea. Already he smelt the tang of salt, and noticed loose strands of seaweed floating on the water. They had reached the tide mark. The tide would carry them swiftly when it was ebbing. It would spare the strength of his men. That would be needed when they turned south. Tonight with a clear sky they could navigate with the stars.

'We have reached the sea, Sigmund,' one of his crew called up to him.

'Aye, men. So I have noticed. I feel its sharpness fill my

chest. I have not smelt the sea for six months. It is the very mead of the gods, is it not men?'

'Aye, Sigmund. And the weather is fair. We should make rapid progress.'

'Aye. Tomorrow night we should sight Shetland. The wind sits fair. We shall sleep well and six men shall mount watch.'

'And shall we capture booty on the Shetlands, Sigmund?'

'No. I go to visit Rolv and show him my wonderful ship.'

'Can you trust Rolv?'

'We trust nobody. You will always sleep with your sword by your side and one eye open.'

It was only in the swell and the slough of the sea that Sigmund the Red knew that his ship was a marvellous thing. Prow strong, it rode the waves firmly answering quickly to the side tiller. He looked down along the lines of the ship, narrowing to the prow and remembered the months of thought and work which had gone into each timber and each cleat, paring each plank back until it was light and supple.

'No finer ship sails, Sigmund. She moves swiftly before the wind,' a crew member called to him.

'Swift as a dolphin, and smooth as a dolphin's hide,' another added.

Behind them the land slipped slowly down below the horizon. Now they had only the vastness of the sea about them. For some this was a feared position. Many ships had ventured too far and had never been seen again. But Sigmund the Red knew how to read the signs in the sea and in the sky. In the event of losing their position he carried with him five ink–black ravens in a timber cage. Released, they would always seek the nearest land position.

The men sang a Viking sea song which seemed to fill the vast sea. It was a dark gutteral song, full of war thirst and they pounded upon their benches. It pleased Sigmund greatly that his crewmen were satisfied with his ship. He opened one of the hold doors and took out a barrel of beer.

He walked among them and filled their mugs many times until they were full of cheer and sang again and again the old songs they had heard from Viking pirates when they were young men. The day remained fair except for one snow shower which came suddenly from the north. For an hour the white blind flakes blew upon them. They drew their cloaks about them and waited for it to pass. Sigmund the Red, without a cloak, stood at the rudder, holding his ship in a firm position, unaffected by the cold. It was deeds such as this, which made him god–like. He seemed to have the very nature of Odin and Thor in his blood. The snow shower passed ahead of them and then it was bright again. The waves were larger now, coming in sullen swells. But the great ship rode them with ease.

When the sun was low in the west, a broad and red shield, and the sea full of moving fire, Sigmund decided to set the sail for the night. His men brought the yard about until it was slanting down across the ship. It would gather sufficient wind to carry it on its course. The sea before them was deep and without shoals. As darkness descended the crewmen wrapped themselves in their large cloaks and lay on the deck. Soon they would be asleep, the sound of the sea in their ears. Sigmund looked at the stars, firm and bright, each one a pointer, directing him to the rich monasteries. Later he fell asleep, his heavy arm across the tiller.

Below him, four crew men looked forward into the night at the eternal blackness of the sea. Sometimes their heads nodded and began to doze but soon they awoke with a quick jerk. Quietly the great ship, newly launched in a deep fjord, resplendent with a wide sail, moved silently down the Northern sea.

CHAPTER 2

The Great Treasure

DIARMUID HAD COME to the island of Iona from Clonmacnoise. It had been a long journey by land and by sea. It had taken six months to reach the small island which was bleak and treeless and the air was heavy with the tang of sea weed and salt. It was a strange new world and for the first few months he was very lonely. Even Declan, the huge soldier monk with his loud laugh and his tangled riddles, could not take his thoughts from Clonmacnoise and his father's dún. Each evening he made his way up to Tor Abb, and sitting on the top of the rocky hill, looked south-west towards Ireland. He watched the flight of birds across the sky, wishing that he had their freedom to move easily from place to place.

One evening, Declan, the warrior monk, had come upon him and discovered him crying.

'Now, what is this I see? A young man crying. Why, I thought that Diarmuid of the Light Hand had banished all his tears the day he left Ireland.'

'No, Declan,' he replied, 'I brought them all with me. I wish I were at home in my father's dún, bringing in the cattle from the prowling wolves. This island is a lonely place and so small. I feel I'm in chains like one of the king's slaves.'

'And what else do you miss?' Declan asked sitting down beside him. Diarmuid felt protected by the presence of this gigantic monk. A wide white scar ran down the left side of his temple and his cheek. It turned purple in cold weather.

'I miss the green fields and the woods and the streams where I fished and the noble Shannon river, which flows so smoothly past Clonmacnoise. I do not like the seagull's call. It is sharp and shrill and pierces my ear and the wind is never gentle here.'

'Soon you will be writing little poems on the side of the great book itself. Brother Ciarán and Brother Cormac did it quite often. I recall one such poem. "Remember Cormac the scribe, who starved at the monastery of Durrow under the hard Abbot Fursey and tasted no ale or wine there. Great are the sufferings of the scribe but greater still are they when he is under a hard abbot." The poem is more famous than the manuscript.'

Declan had many stories about the two brothers: 'They could never get on. Cormac was small and fidgety and his mind was never at rest. He could not sit at a manuscript for more than an hour and then he was up and walking over and back and scratching the side of his head bitterly complaining about something or other. Ciarán was large and slow and loved nothing more than filling in colours in manuscripts. They never let him touch the large important works. He could destroy in an hour what it took a year to fashion. Well, one day a fight broke out in the scriptorium between the two. Cormac poured an inkhorn full of black ink on Ciarán's head, and Ciarán who was separating yokes from whites, started throwing eggs at Cormac. Then Cormac chased Ciarán all around the monastery until the abbot came up with them. They were banished from Iona.'

The story had cheered Diarmuid. He knew that home sickness would come upon him again. He would climb the hill and think of the small woods where the blackbird sang, where the horizons were large and the sea did not boom in his ears at night.

Declan looked towards the south. The sky was crowded with grey clouds. They could see the sea darkening. Brother Sixtus, some distance out from the island, had noticed the change in the weather. He payed out his net rapidly, took the oars and began to row shorewards. They had several curraghs in the small coves about the island. The monastery partly lived off the sea. Every morning some of the brothers set out in the small curraghs to check the night lines and the nets. One monk cured the fish. They became hard as leather in the wind and Brother Cormac once said that they could be used in manuscripts. To prove that he was correct, he had made out some rough designs on the cured fish and coloured them with greens and red.

'We better hasten back to the monastery,' Brother Declan said, 'It is different with Brother Sixtus. Sea and rain are his natural elements. He is happier on the sea than on the land.'

'His hand is upon the book,' Diarmuid said. 'His small fish and cats, birds and men give the book life.'

'And so it is.'

Brother Sixtus worked out his designs for the Great Book in his curragh. When he came ashore, he hastened to the scriptorium and worked rapidly and then disappeared again. Like Declan, he wished that the book were finished. He feared the Viking raiders from the North. When finished, it would be the most wonderful book in the world, the Book of Iona. It would surpass even the Book of Lindisfarne.

They moved down quickly from the hill. Declan looked at the monastery beneath them.

'The monastery is not safe,' he said. His voice was dark. The laughter had left his face. It was the voice of the soldier which he had tried to subdue on Tiree during his long penance. He could never forget his past. He had been the highest paid kern in his day, sought by the princes and kings of Ireland and Scotland to lead men into battle. Now his sword, sheathed in a scabbard of leather, hung on the walls of the abbot's cell.

They stopped for a moment and looked at the unprotected monastery. It was surrounded by earthen ditches thrown up by the monks over the centuries. Within the earthen ditch stood the cells of the monks, sometimes square and thatched, sometimes circular like beehives, with their walls of daub and wattles, covered with lime which seemed to glow with inner light even in the rain. In the centre of the enclosure stood the oak walled chapel with its golden thatch. Running along the eastern wall were the workshops. Here the stone masons and the smiths worked. Beside these stood the workshops of the miller, the tanner, the gardener and the baker. Standing alone, away from the other buildings, was the scriptorium with its large windows to let in the light from the south. When the wind blew firmly from this direction, they had to shutter the openings and work by tallow light.

'Do you not see how it is exposed? Stone walls should be thrown up about it. We should set a constant guard in a tower. Some marauder could destroy all our work.'

'Surely they would not destroy the Book. Our work must not be interrupted.'

'You do not know the ways of the warriors. You are a boy

of fourteen. I know the marauder's mind.'

They talked as they passed down the path from the hill, Declan looking behind him at the rain clouds driving up from the south. He would be confined to his cell for the evening. All his life he had been a wanderer, going from army to army, from prince to prince. He hated the small, confined space of his cell. Sometimes he felt the urge to tear it down. He had to keep a rein on his vast energies.

On fine days, he worked in the large garden pulling the rough plough, the rope bound to his waist. This was one of the penances set upon him to break his warlike spirit. He had rebelled many times.

'Brother Amedy treats me like a horse,' he told the abbot. 'I'll turn on him, lord abbot, and you will have blood on your hands.'

The abbot, for some wise reason, never lifted the penance.

'You will have to bear the heavy burden, Brother Declan. Someday it will be lifted.'

'I cannot continue,' he had told him. 'The island is a prison. I walk and walk and try to burn off my angers but they still come in sea surges.'

The abbot now watched them as they entered the enclosure from his small cell beside the gate. He worried about Declan and he worried about Diarmuid. Perhaps Diarmuid had been too young to bring to the monastery. He was a frail delicate youth, his features fine, his fingers long and sensitive. He had come to Iona from the scriptorium of Clonmacnoise to work on the great book. By the age of twelve, he had copied his first psalter. At fourteen, he was the most accomplished scribe in the scriptorium. He could grasp a picture totally at a single glance, and reproduce it swiftly and with accuracy.

His health was frail. During the damp months his chest was raked with a hard cough. The abbot had often warmed mead for him and brought it to his cell with herbs from the island to dissolve the phlegm which was choking him. Twice they had put him in the sweat house to draw away the mucus.

The abbot carried many worries in his mind. The monastery had grown too rapidly during the last fifteen years. There was constant coming and going between it and the mainland. The workshops had to be supplied with precious metal and stones, the scriptorium with vellum and pigment. Many of the pigments could be made locally but others came from the very borders of the known world, particularly ultramarine which was more valuable than gold. He wondered if he had been too ambitious setting out to create the most beautiful book in the world. He had travelled to many monasteries and studied their manuscripts before he had embarked upon the project. His journeys had taken him down the coast to England and from there to Northern France in the large curragh with its double sails. He had gathered on the island the best artists he could find. One monk had travelled from Egypt. Now after fifteen years they were nearing the end. Three more years and it would be finished and bound in ornamental covers of gold and precious stones.

Brother Declan had told him that peace was a fragile thing and he had replied, 'we shall be granted peace. No Scottish prince will descend upon the island. The princes of Scotland consider it an honour to be buried here, close to Columcille himself.'

'It is not Scottish Princes I worry about, lord abbot, but the menace from the North.'

'We pay tribute to Rolv of Shetland. Each year he receives the Danegeld. It buys us our peace.'

'His power could fail. He may control the seas for the moment but others will move out from the fjords.' Declan spoke with a firm voice and a knowledge of the sea thieves' heart.

'Go inland, lord abbot, away from the rivers. Go to a lonely glen. In one year we could build a monastery larger than Iona and with ten masons I could raise the ramparts large enough to keep any enemy at bay.'

'Your mind is too much on thoughts of war, Brother Declan. You still have not forgotten your old calling. I have heard you cry out the battle cries in your sleep.'

'My thoughts are not on war. I am a practical man and I know what is happening.'

Already travellers coming from the North were carrying strange stories with them. In the beginning they were just rumours. But as the summer heightened, the rumours seemed to carry some truth. One traveller had seen a strange ship, more like a serpent than a ship, make its way under single sail through the Orkney islands. It was long and sleek and moved swiftly through the water. It was manned by expert oarsmen. Standing at the prow of this swift ship stood a fierce sailor, in a tunic of leather, studded with iron disks. His beard and the long hair which escaped beneath his horned helmet were of flaming red.

Another traveller had witnessed a village put to the torch, the smoke passing out over the sea. Women and men had been carried down to the ship as prisoners.

There were strange stirrings in the north. Once the abbot had feared the harsh winters and looked to the advent of summer, when the scribes could work out of door. They often left the most delicate ornamentation for the summer time, when their hands were firm. Now he wished for the winter time with its storms and tempests which threw up a protection around the island.

He wondered if they should abandon the sacred place. He would have to come to some decision. What should he do if the book and the cover were endangered? He would not see it destroyed. It was a work he could not hasten. Many single illuminated pages had yet to be bound into the text, there were many pages of script to be written.

He looked at Brother Declan's sword hanging on the wall in its leather scabbard. There were probably rust stains upon the blade but it was still a fine sword. Should he now return it to Brother Declan and tell him that the time was ripe to take the book from the island to some inland monastery, where it could be finished in peace, surrounded by birdsong?

He watched the rain fall on the enclosure. It was a grey sad rain. He wondered about this serpent shaped Viking ship which was moving so rapidly upon the northern seas.

CHAPTER 3

Treachery

MORNING CAME GRADUALLY out of the east. At first, deep grey filtered through the clouds, later it became silver. It was a fresh morning and a firm breeze carried the ship along. The crew stirred from their sleep, casting back their heavy cloaks. They rubbed their eyes, and stretched their backs which were stiff from the timbers. They looked at the sea. It stretched endlessly in all directions.

Sigmund was awake before the crew. He stood at the rudder, his eye sharp for the movements of birds. He knew that he was on direct course for the Shetland Islands. Rolv of Shetland lived there. He had sailed once under him. Now he wished to show him the magnificent ship he possessed, better than any of Rolv's protection vessels, which brought the southern ships through the dangerous northern waters. A doubtful friendship existed between the two leaders.

When the men had eaten their rough breakfast of bread and meat, he called out: 'Bring down the sail. I wish to test the speed of the ship on the open sea.'

Still sleepy, they pushed the oars into the oar ports and waited for the drum beat. Sigmund hit the drum with his clenched fist. The men began to row. Now he would test their endurance. He quickened the drum beat. The men responded with their oars. The ship moved quickly across the waves. The men's bodies moved forwards and backwards together to an even rhythm. Soon sweat was pouring down their faces, their muscles bulging with pain. No sea captain had ever required them to move so quickly and for so long a time. Was it true, they asked themselves, that this Sigmund was as cruel and treacherous as his reputation, laughing with them in the evening, using them like slaves in the morning time? They looked up at him expecting him to stop the pounding of the drum, but he looked at each pair of eyes, seeking any sign of mutiny. Finally their rhythm broke and their oars tangled.

'You are not oarsmen,' he roared. 'Why, the women in the village would hold out longer.'

'You drive us beyond our limits, Sigmund,' one of them said.

'You will row longer distances and at greater speeds before Sigmund the Red is finished with you.'

Sigmund the Red had a purpose in putting the crewmen through such a gruelling test. They learned what manner of man he was. He had also discovered which members of his crew would first grow mutinous.

All that day, under sail, they passed down the north sea. As the sun entered its third quarter, he noticed island birds for the first time. Slowly land began to rise out of the horizon. It was the island of Unst. He had brought his crew and ship easily and swiftly through a night and a day over the sea and struck the island directly. His bearings had been correct.

'Who will say that Sigmund the Red is not a great navigator? Ahead lies the island of Unst. We came out of the great sea and reached it directly, not searching for it like fools of captains who can not judge the signs in the sky and on the sea. Who is the greatest of all the captains who sail the seas?'

'Sigmund the Red!' They called.

'We shall prosper under Sigmund.

They quickly forgot that they were tired. Their interest was now upon the island which was growing out of the sea. Small hills and bays became definite.

'We will sail to Muckle Row with our sail filled with

wind, our shields glinting in the sun.

Under full sail they moved about the islands of Unst and Yell. To the north of Papa Stour they swung directly east. Ahead lay Muckle Row and the settlement of Rolv of Shetland.

Soon they could make out smoke drifting from the settlement. As they drew closer, they could see the stone houses huddled together and close to the shore. As they neared the settlement, they could see cattle and sheep grazing on a stretch of grass directly above the shore.

People were running along the shore waving. They recognised the Viking ship and knew that a kinsman had arrived. A boat put out from the shore.

'Ah, it is Sigmund the Red I see,' Rolv of Shetland called from the boat. 'You are the captain of a fine ship, and not like the ship of Ulick the Fair, which was slow and heavy on the water.'

'This ship, Rolv, is the finest ship which ever took the sea road from the north,' Sigmund boasted.

Rolv ordered his men to row about the ship. He looked at each line and plank. She was swifter than any of his ships. She could be a danger to his convoys. He must find out more of Sigmund the Red's plans. He was dangerous and his mind filled with treachery.

'You stay with us tonight. You know the old saying, When a guest arrives, chilled to the very heart, from his sea journey, he needs fire, food and drink. So hasten ashore. Your men can follow.'

When they reached the shore they walked through the village, talking rapidly and trying to catch up with the events of the past years. Sigmund took note of the settlement. The houses were built of flat stone and Rolv had raised many stone walls for his cattle.

'You have settled down, Rolv. You are a petty prince here.'

'You should pick out some good land, Sigmund, and settle down.'

'No, I will always follow the call of the sea.

Rolv's feast

They entered a large house. It was furnished with tables and chairs. The window was made from animal membrane. It was a comfortable house and soon the women brought them wooden plates filled with food. They took the drinking horns which were filled with mead and toasted each other.

'This is rich drink, Rolv.' Sigmund told him.

'The wine comes from the south, the honey from the north.'

They drank for a long time and talked of the days when they sailed together. They did not feel the time pass. Evening gradually became night.

Later, arm in arm and singing old songs of the sea, they made their way to the guest house. Already there was noise from within the hall. Sigmund entered. His eyes caught the glint of silver bowls and dishes on the tables. Probably stolen from some monastery or other, Sigmund thought.

'You set a table fit for a king, Rolv,' he said.

'We often eat thus and think it no great thing. In the north you do not eat as well or dwell in such long and large houses.'

The insult was lost on the crew who were savaging ox meat and drinking beer. Sigmund resisted the desire to plunge a dagger in Rolv's back and pillage the island.

He settled into the meal drinking the wine and carving large sweet slices of meat from the ox haunches. He would be at peace with Rolv for the moment. While they ate, a poet chanted the old sagas which told of voyages to distant lands.

'Someday the adventures of Sigmund the Red will be sung by the poets. None greater sails the sea. No greater is found on land,' one of his crew called from the bottom of the table. 'We fear no enemy. Even this island could be taken by Sigmund were he not a friend to Rolv.'

Rolv glanced suspiciously down the table. He did not trust Sigmund. He had seen him once kill his own companions in a drunken brawl. He would answer the braggard.

'There is one greater than Sigmund,' he told them. 'He is a soldier monk called Declan. Even in Shetland the fame of his deeds are known. No one greater wields the double edged sword.'

'And where can we find this strange monk?' they asked.

'Some say in Ireland, some say in Iona where they are making the most beautiful book in the world.'

'And does he use his sword as a quill?' they laughed.

'No, he is a penitent. He prays to be forgiven for his wicked deeds.'

'Let me come up with this fellow,' Sigmund said, 'and I will make him worship at the idol of Thor I carry on my ship.'

They continued to boast long into the night. When they were drunk they slid onto the floor. Only Sigmund the Red and Rolv remained.

'I shall prosper at sea,' Sigmund told Rolv. 'You are a land man. You have lost the power.'

'You are a maurauder,' Rolv said drunkenly. 'I claim the danegeld. I give protection to the rich ships. Why at this very moment, a ship is sailing up the seas from the south worth a king's ransom.'

'And where lies this ship now, Rolv?'

'Such secrets lie in my heart. Sigmund will not have such secrets.'

Sigmund could not prize open the rich secret. However he played a clever chance. He fell forward on his face and pretended to sleep. Listening, he heard Rolv mutter: 'The route, the golden route, given to a red maurauder. He wishes to know where the Frisian ship hides in the Isle of Coll waiting for the Viking guard ship. Five days hence my ships shall be there.'

Sigmund snored loudly, secure in the knowledge that a prize worth a king's ransom would soon be his.

Next day, heavy of head, his crew set out on their journey of three days to Coll. They passed down the North Minch, and moved into the Little Minch. Then they turned south-east and anchored at the island of Rhum. They sacked an island village, set fire to the houses, and provisioned themselves for two days. Then they waited for the fourth day.

Meanwhile on the island of Coll, the Dorstead ship was at anchor in a small bay. It was protected from the sea by two hillocks, which guarded the entrance.

Roland Dirk, was anxious that the Viking ships, which would accompany them to the Baltic, would soon arrive. He had no wish to eat wild goat or fish. He had been brought up in civilized towns of the south and he hated the harshness of the weather and the landscape. Above all he was suspicious of the Vikings. But the rewards were worth the chance. Three more journeys into the North Seas and he would be a rich man. In return for his Byzantine silks and brocades and his Frisian cloth he would receive valuable furs and amber. Already he had delivered some precious ultramarine pigments at the monastery of Iona. The very gold he had received would help him pay the Vikings for safe passage. He had moored his ship in this safe and secret harbour two days previously.

They had camped on the shore and pitched their coloured tents in a sheltered place. They had lit a fire and were preparing an evening meal. Some of his crew remained on board the ship to keep watch.

It was twilight when the Viking ship, carrying the emblem of the Sea Dragon, sailed between the small hills and into the harbour. It appeared suddenly out of the dusk and caught them by surprise. On the prow stood the tall wild figure of a Viking calling orders to his men.

'The ship has arrived.' A crewman called to Roland Dirk on the shore. He looked into the gathering darkness. Roland Dirk knew instantly that this was not the ship he had been expecting.

'Run for your lives,' he called to his men. 'It is a pirate ship. We are ruined.'

The Vikings bore down upon the ship. There was blood

lust in their eyes. They clambered on board, calling out their frightening war cries. Most savage, and fearful of all was the red haired Viking. His eyes burned bright with battle fury. He cut at a Flemish sailor with his sword. It slashed his jerkin and slit a purse which contained gold coins. They clattered onto the deck. The blow should have carried on into his body. He knew that he was wounded. He staggered across the ship and fell overboard.

'Is he dead?' Roared Sigmund.

'If he is not, he will be. It was a deadly blow to the side. He will bleed to death.'

'They all must die. We cannot leave anyone to tell the story. Kill them before you throw them overboard.'

The Flemish sailor lay inert among the floating bodies about him. He could feel the smart of sea salt in his wound.

The battle for the ship was soon over.

'Should we collect the bodies and bury them?' A crew member asked Sigmund.

'Let the sea have them. The tides will wash them up on different shores. Nobody will ever know who they were or where they came from.'

'Should we search their pockets?'

'No, there is wealth enough on the ship.'

Now it was dark. Looking up, the Flemish sailor could see the torches move up and down the ship as they examined the cargo. He listened to their talk for he partly understood it. He could hear the words 'wine and silk' mentioned several times. Later they would discover the gold hidden under the deck.

They had broken open some of the wine casks and were drinking them. Wounded and cold, he thought how the rich wine of Burgundy, so carefully matured in cellars, was abused by the heathen. It would quickly set them drunk. Now somebody had discovered the gold.

'Sigmund,' they called, 'We have found gold beneath the deck. Long bars of gold. There is a king's ransom here.'

There was much pledging of trusts and wine promises

above him. He must now move. As he looked up he could see Sigmund's face caught by torch light. He held a small cask of wine in his hand. He was speaking to one of his crew.

'Tomorrow we will comb the island for survivors. There must be no survivors to carry the news back to Rolv. Then we will move on the monastery of Iona. It is a short journey from here.'

Quietly the Flemish sailor swam to where a small boat lay some yards from the ship. He cut the rope with his dagger. Then, floating on his back, he drew it away from the ship. This was his only means of escape. The current carried both himself and the boat towards the open sea. He had lost a great amount of blood. Gripping the side of the small boat and gathering his remaining strength he dragged himself aboard. He weakened quickly and lay unconscious on the bottom of the boat.

Abandoned to the whims of the sea, the small boat was first carried east by the current and then southwards.

Three days the Vikings remained on the island. Their task was difficult. The island was full of coves and inlets. All who were captured were put to the sword. When all had been accounted for they decided to sail immediately from the island.

'Burn the ship,' Sigmund ordered, 'She is a slow ship and would be recognized.'

They set the ship on fire and moved away from her. They watched as the flames caught the riggings and the sail which they had hoisted. It fell flaming into the body of the ship which then caught fire. Soon the timbers were crackling in flame, a huge pall of smoke moving out over the island. Satisfied that they had accomplished their task, they moved out of the small harbour. They sailed in the direction of Iona. If Sigmund's raid on Iona was successful, then he would have enough riches to fit another ship and sail southwards the following summer.

'We will search out Iona,' he called. 'There are riches

there for us all. And perhaps we will meet this strange soldier monk called Declan. I am sure that prayer and fasting have left him weak. He will worship at the altar of Thor.'

They moved down the seas from the island of Coll. Next morning Rolv's ship arrived at the island. They discovered the burnt shell of the ship, and came upon the slaughtered sailors.

'The hand of Sigmund the Red is evident here,' the two sea captains agreed. 'He has betrayed the confidence of Rolv. We shall take council and then one of us shall return to the Shetlands. The other shall stalk the ship of Sigmund.'

They knew that Rolv would settle this score with Sigmund the Red. They were now enemies.

CHAPTER 4

Setting a Trap

THE BELL FOR MORNING PRAYER rang out over Iona.
Brother Sixtus was already at the door of his cell.

'Thank the Lord for a silver sky,' he chanted. 'May he
temper the air, give repose to the dead, peace to the kings
and help seafarers on their way across the endless sea.'

The air was full of sea scents. The breath of summer was
on the island, carrying with it perfume from the small
flowers and the heather.

His cat, Secundius, was milking the morning light with
his paws. He had brought him as a kitten from Ireland and
he had made his appearance many times in the great book.
He was very much alive there, bounding over the letters,
getting entangled in them and substituting his body for
them to relieve tedium.

The Coptic monk, all the way from the edge of the known
world, a place of barren sand hills, had objected to the
presence of Secundius in so sacred a book. The matter had
been brought to Connachtach, the abbot.

'This is a very serious book, lord abbot,' the Coptic monk
began. 'At night time I have visions of what great drawing
should be placed on the vellum. I tremble in the presence
of the book. But Brother Sixtus comes in from the sea,
takes down one of the pages, draws cats and hens and
leaves laughing. Some of the pages even smell of fish.'

The charity of Sixtus was strained. The Copt was serious.
But then, Sixtus reflected, he came from the Eastern Church,
and he had made a long sea journey to work on the book.

His health was frail and he wore a double cloak. He was in a strange land and his body was raked by fevers. Sixtus had let him complain, and endured the heavy penance that was imposed upon him by the abbot. He was forbidden to sail on the sea for six weeks. During that time he had walked about the island, like a chained slave, knowing that shoals of herring were moving down past the island and that the other monks did not know where to set the nets or lobster pots.

But on this bright summer's morning his penance was only a memory and he had forgiven the Copt. He made his way to the chapel with the others. The gospel told of Peter fishing the lake of Galilee and catching nothing. Maybe he was a bad fisherman, like some of the monks, Sixtus thought. Then he thought of his own nets and soon his mind was at sea.

Abbot Connachtach, sitting on his abbot's chair, and looking down upon his monks, wondered for their safety, and for the safety of the great book. The island was too exposed to the Viking maurauders, and Rolv of Shetland might not be able to protect them. The raid on the holy island of Lindisfarne was fresh in his mind. At the end of the prayers he gave them his blessing and they left the church and set about their work. The cook went to the kitchen and warmed the porridge. Brother John poured milk into wooden mugs. Brother Loman gutted fish down at the sea shore. Others let out the cattle and the hens and gathered the eggs. The morning was always a busy time and a hundred things needed attention.

Diarmuid prayed that his hand would be steady as he made his way to the large scriptorium after breakfast. Perhaps today the scribes might work out of doors. There were certain sections of the Chi Rho page which could only be worked on in intense light.

He lifted the wooden latch on the door and entered the scriptorium. It was a large wide building with windows of animal membrane to let in the light on cold days. It was filled with the smell of oak gall, and the scent of vellum - on the northern wall which never caught the sun, ranged the leather satchels that hung from wooden pegs. There were at least forty satchels, each containing the manuscripts of the monastery. They sent their psalters to other monasteries in exchange for gold, which paid for the pigments. The young scribes worked at the western end of the room. Their job was tedious for they had to cramp as much miniscule writing as possible onto the small vellum sheets, occasionally daring to insert an ornamental letter at the beginning of a chapter.

Diarmuid stood in the golden silence of the room. It was a noble place. Strong oak beams carried the high thatch. The walls were limed to bring brightness into the room. Here the scribes talked only in hushed voices. The fame of this room had travelled to all the monasteries.

In the eastern part of the building, the scribes and illuminators worked on the greatest Gospel book which had ever been created. Diarmuid knew that he was in the company of the greatest scribes, illuminators and portrait painters in the world when he worked in this part of the scriptorium. Connachtach had gathered them from all over Ireland, England and Scotland, each monk superb at his work. Diarmuid and Connachtach alone knew where every page of the book lay in the satchels. It was Diarmuid's duty to keep the pages in order, to make certain that the inks were dry before replacing the pages in their satchels. When finished – that is, pressed and bound and carrying the cover of gold upon which they were now working – it would contain over three hundred and sixty pages.

He set out the compasses, the triangles of copper, the metal rulers, and the fine stylii with their sharp points for ruling and tracing. Then he set out one hundred copper stencils, each carrying a different shape. 'And now for the great moment,' he thought to himself. He went over to the most important satchel of all. He examined his fingers before he opened it. Certain that they were clean, he took out the Chi Rho page and placed it reverently on a square of hard leather in order that the grainy timber would not make an impress upon it. Brother Paul, once a metal worker, had spent two years on this page. Now it was almost finished. The work had been so intricate and delicate that Paul was now almost blind. Each morning he was led to the scriptorium and placed at his desk. He would bend down and, with his eyes two inches from the page, work on the delicate traceries, stretching out his hand and calling for quills and pigments which were handed to him by a monk who always stood by. Diarmuid gazed down in awe upon the page.

'You think that it is more wonderful than the carpet page?' A voice whispered at his shoulder. It was one of the young scribes whom he had not noticed enter.

'Oh, by far, by far,' Diarmuid said, his eyes intent upon the page.

'But they are done by the same hand.'

'I know, but in the carpet page you have only ornaments, very skillful ornaments. This page is free. The eye never tires of it. It would have run wild in a lesser artist's hands. See how the purples and reds on the two letters hold it together and give it strength. It is controlled from within.'

'I do not understand.'

'Brother Paul drew it on the sand a thousand times before he traced it on wax. They say that the water came up about his feet as he looked at it and when it was erased from the sand he thought that it was still there.'

'I never knew that.'

'There are lots of strange things about this book which you will never know. Brother Sergius, the Coptic monk, was assaulted by the devil when he drew the temptation scene.'

'That's the page with the black ugly devil?'

'Yes. And do you know that the portrait painter spent a

The work of the monastery

day and a night and a day in the scriptorium, unaware of the passage of time while they held tallow candles to give him light.'

He continued to look at the page. Who would ever understand the whole tangle of the page, the mystical meaning of each line, of the butterfly high up in the page, the small black otter in the cave at the bottom, the cats and kittens holding the white bread?

The animals and the butterfly were the work of Brother Sixtus. He had protested that he was unworthy to touch such a page and that he could not draw butterflies, so the abbot had to order him to do it.

'It's the tightest work I ever did,' he boasted afterwards. 'It took me a whole week to figure out how I was going to put the otter in the cave and I spent twenty days looking at butterflies in the meadow before I did the butterfly at the top. My hands trembled each time I touched the page. They say I shall be remembered for ever.'

But there was much more to the page and only Diarmuid and a few others knew its meaning.

While Diarmuid prepared the manuscript, the abbot was consulting with his advisors. He listened to them for a long time, before speaking: 'I have come to the following decision. The book must be protected. It is already too valuable. It must be removed from the island. It is almost finished now. We have completed our great undertaking.'

'We have lived for the book and would gladly die for it. Let it remain,' came a quick, warm response.

'No. It must be taken from the island. Perhaps later it will be returned if these dark clouds gathering in the north pass away. All the scribes will return to Ireland. Brother Sixtus will take them across the seas in his large hide boat. I am placing Diarmuid in charge of the satchels. He is very young I know, but he alone knows the total scheme of the book.'

'They will need protection,' a monk remarked.

'I know. I am giving Brother Declan back his sword.'

'But once he feels it in his hand, all his old battle angers may return. Ten years he has tried to burn out these angers. He may renege upon his vows and return to the field of carnage,' another warned.

'I have turned these things over in my mind. We must take chances in times like these.' And with that the meeting was over. He sent for Diarmuid at the scriptorium. He made his way to the abbot's cell.

'You shall soon be returning to Ireland,' Connachtach began.

'Have I displeased you with my work, lord abbot?'

'No, Diarmuid. You came here as a boy and you are still very young. Into your charge I am giving the great book. You must take it to Ireland. It shall be finished in the most peaceful of surroundings.'

'Will you not travel with us, lord abbot?'

'No, Diarmuid. You are now in charge of the great work. Find a quiet valley through which streams run, and where birds sing in cloistral woods. You know all that is to be known about the book. All the scribes and illuminators will go with you. Take special care of Brother Paul for he is very old now, a master above all masters. Bring the news I gave you to the scriptorium and prepare for departure.'

Brother Declan, yoked to a plough, had been working in the fields all morning, when he was called. He was always called to the abbot's cell when there was trouble. 'It is hard to be perfect,' he thought. 'No matter how I try, there is always something wrong.' He left the half-ploughed field and made his way to the abbot's cell.

'Do your shoulders ache, Brother Declan?' The abbot asked.

'The rope often cuts into them, lord abbot, but I offer the pain for those I killed in battle.'

'Brother Declan, would you ever take the sword in your hand again?'

'No, lord abbot. I gave you my promise and I did my penance. Let it rust in its scabbard on the wall.'

'Well, Declan, I am handing you back the sword.'

'I don't want it, my lord. Do not send me from the monastery. No one wants an old soldier and I fear that if I touch the handle all my old war urges will return.'

'Declan, we fear that the Vikings will descend upon the island. We are sending the great book to Ireland under the care of Diarmuid. You must protect it.'

'And you, my lord abbot, must protect the island.'

'How can one protect such an exposed place?'

'I have been drawing up battle plans. In battle, lord abbot, there is rarely luck, only plans and deceit. I will build a furze and heather wall with openings on the sea shore and set traps for the maraurders.'

'But we are men of peace, Declan.'

'Men of peace within, my lord, but men of war outside. You owe it to your monks. You will not have them cut down like grass.'

'Prepare the defences, Declan.' He then stood up and went over to the wall where the famous sword hung. He grasped the scabbard in both hands and took it down.

'Take it,' the abbot said.

'No,' Declan resisted.

'I order you. Defend the book and all who sail with Brother Sixtus.'

His hands shook as he took the sword scabbard with its sword.

'Draw it. See if it is still fit for service.'

Declan cramped his fingers several times to break the stiffness of the years. Then he placed his hand on the golden hilt. Almost immediately he felt some spirit within him pass down into the sword as if they carried the same blood. He was afraid to awake it from its long sleep. It might be rusty and aged, for a sword, like a man, grew old. Slowly he eased it out of the leather scabbard. The blade was stippled with rust spots but otherwise it was silver bright, sharp at the edges, ridged in the middle. The years had not weakened it. It was a huge sword.

'Let us go outside and see if you can still use this great sword. I have heard much about your speed and exactness.'

They went outside the enclosure to a large single post which was set in the ground.

'Now let me see you bury the sword in the post.'

'It needs to be honed, lord abbot,'

'Never mind your excuses.'

'What if I give the battle roar?' he asked.

'Give the battle roar. The brothers will think you are having one of your nightmares.' The abbot smiled.

Declan held the sword directly in front of him. His face tightened in concentration as if he were praying to some god of war. In frenzy he rushed at the post screaming out his battle cry. The sword sang in the air, twisting and turning to subtle wrist work. The sword movement was circular and unbroken. When the abbot looked at the post it had been sliced evenly eight times.

'You have made me a pagan, Connachtach. It is as if I had never come to Iona. I am slower than I was. I know from the sword hum.'

Connachtach looked at the severed post. He had under-estimated Declan's virtue. Few men had ever made the sacrifices he had made. For a proud soldier with such sword craft to pull a monastery plough must have been a galling penance. 'Now, Declan, we must fortify the monastery. One half-hour may give us a chance to escape to the main land. I will sound the bell and call the monks from the fields.'

Word had quickly passed through the monastery that the book was to be taken from the island. The news was received with disbelief. They whispered among themselves when they saw Declan with his scabbard belt buckled over his rough monastery garb and the golden hilt showing above the scabbard. He would turn the monastery into an army camp. He gathered the monks about him and in a harsh soldierly voice ordered them to gather the island furze and heather and bring them to the shore. Others he ordered to dig large pits in squares marked out with his sword, Others he ordered to take every pole they could find and point it spear sharp.

By evening the satchels containing the great book and the half-finished cover were packed. Near the beach, sharp poles had been driven into the pits and the pits covered with scraws.

'Tallow lights must burn beside the furze walls,' Declan told them. 'I will place guards. Keep an eye to the straits.'

He walked beside the wall and examined his fortifications. He was pleased with the work. He had played the same trick once before when he had found himself in a tight corner.

Meanwhile Brother Sixtus was unaware of the preparations on the island. He was far out to sea and the sound of the bell was not carried over the waters. He had set his nets for the herring shoals and now he waited for them to pass down by the island. His eyes were always to the sea and the sky. There were clouds to the south but they did not carry rain. The sea was even.

It was towards evening that he noticed the strange boat on the waters some distance from him. He knew from its lines that it was a boat from the south. He hoisted his sail and abandoned the nets. His leather boat rode rapidly over the waves towards the strange craft. He circled about it and drew up alongside and looked in. On the floor of the boat a crew member of Roland Dirk's ship lay dying, a pool of blood at his side. He climbed across to the boat and saw that the man was still alive. He fetched the leather pouch of spring water which he always carried and lifting the man's head gave him a drink. The man's eyes stared in front of him as if witnessing some vision or other. He kept on repeating, 'Sigmund the Red. Sigmund the Red. Iona. Iona. Flee. Flee.' Sixtus realised that only Brother Fiachra could stop the bleeding. He secured the boat to his own, hoisted his sail and headed back towards the island. Behind him he could hear the man groaning. It was getting dark now. The wind was not strong in the sail and the progress was slow. It was night when he reached the small cove. He rushed across the fields calling for help.

He could not understand what was happening in the enclosure. He rushed to the abbot's cell. It was empty. He rushed down to the sea front and found Connachtach.

'I need help, lord abbot. I discovered a boat at sea with a dying man. He is a crew member of Roland Dirk's ship. He talks of Sigmund the Red and Iona.'

Connachtach knew at that moment that he had taken the correct decision.

'Bring Fiachra with you to the cove and carry the stranger to the guest house.'

By the time they reached the small cove, the crew man was dead. They put him on the rough stretcher and stumbling in the dark they brought him to the small mortuary where they laid out the monks when they died. They crossed his arms and closed his eyes.

It was completely dark now. All preparations to defend the monastery had been made. Filled with fear, the monks returned to their cells, hoping the maurauders would not descend upon the peaceful island. Declan, having set the watch, went to his cell and slept with the sword in his hand. Diarmuid slept with the satchel straps upon his shoulders. Connachtach had told Sixtus of his plans. Sixtus immediately set off across the island to prepare the two-masted boat. It was a still night, the stars firm and bright. Sixtus had often sailed by these stars across unknown seas. He wondered if Sigmund the Red was following the sea paths guided by the same stars.

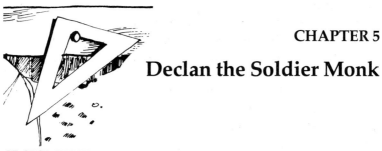

CHAPTER 5

Declan the Soldier Monk

IF SIGMUND THE RED HAD ANY DOUBTS over his attack on the merchant ship, he kept them to himself. He could outstrip any ship Rolv of Shetland would send against him.

His crew were happy for the moment. They were pleased with the booty. But he must keep his eye on Gissur the Bald. There was treason in his eyes and he sailed with six of his villagers.

They travelled south east towards Mull. They would rest here for the night and sail for the island of Iona in the early morning light. They set up their camp beneath a cliff, had their night meal and went to sleep. It was a warm night and Sigmund thought that it would be good for a man to settle in a hospitable climate and not return to Norway to be ice bound for five months of the year, where the earth was thin and miserly, the food harsh. The sound of the sea was gentle here, not rough and confused by tempests.

At first light his men were awake. They gathered their weapons and rough blankets and waded out towards the ship. It rested proud and ferocious on the water. Its very appearance would terrify the soft monks.

ON IONA, THE MONKS had kept watch all night. Mist began to close in about them and blot out the stars during the second watch. Behind the rampart of furze and heather the tallow candles burned in clay vessels. They prayed that they might be protected from the idol worshippers from the north. The mist rolling up from the south might hide the island.

Sixtus had made many journeys across the island. He had strapped the masts and the sails to the horse and brought them to where the large boat lay in the cove. He set the masts and tied the sail to the yardarm so that it could be hoisted with ease. He set the steering paddle in the frame and tightened and secured all ropes. Later he brought provisions and water and placed them in the centre of the boat for ballast.

As he journeyed across the island, he planned what course he would follow down the seas towards Ireland. He wondered if he should dash directly out into the open sea or slip between the islands and along the coast and then with advantageous winds make a swift night journey across the North Channel. The open seas were dangerous during the summer months; the light lay too long upon the waves and the Viking ships could move more rapidly than his leather boat.

While Sixtus was making the final preparations, Sigmund approached the island. He came slowly through the mist. He would catch the monks by surprise. Grasping the tiller and trimming the sail to the wind, he edged in towards the shore. His eyes peered into the mist seeking the monastery settlement. Below him, his men were strapping their shields to their arms, cleaning their sword blades on their tunics as they often did, to pass the time and steady their nerves.

Out of the mist loomed the monastery, with its thatched roofs. There were many buildings. It was larger than he had expected. As he swung the ship in towards the shore, he noticed the high walls of furze and heather with the five gaps between them. He wondered about them for a moment. There was no sound from the monastery.

Declan had been wakened early. He always slept well before battle. He had been trained to catch sleep in open fields, on mountain sides, even on snow. While he slept, strength gathered within him.

'Have they been sighted?' he asked the monk who had wakened him.

'No. A mist is thickening about the island.

'Have the candles been covered?'

'Yes.'

'They must be kept burning at all costs. Have you collected the swords?'

'We could only discover ten.'

'What is ten against a Viking ship? I told the abbot an age ago I would train the monks in the use of arms but he would not listen to me.'

'We are men of peace.'

'Men of peace should have more sense.'

He prayed for a short time on the floor of his cell. Then he bound his scabbard belt about him and went to the fortifications.

He examined the ten swords. They were blunt and rusty. He ordered one of the monks to fetch every scythe in the monastery. They could handle the scythes better than swords. While he walked along his line of defence, he continued to open and close his hands in order to make his fingers supple. At other times he whipped the sword from the scabbard and cut at the air, listening to the sword note.

'You have not forgotten the skills of battle,' Diarmuid said to him.

'I thought perhaps I had but once I grasped my sword I knew that I was wrong. Every trick and turn and skill was lurking at the back of my mind.'

'Shall we get the great book to Ireland, Declan?'

'We will. I'll fight the battles on the land. Let Sixtus bear us safely across the sea.'

He welcomed the mist which was about the island. It was to his advantage. The monks could move quickly to the mainland under cover. Fifty would wait and fight.

The monks came to Connachtach and he gave them a final blessing. They departed in silence for the small coves.

Diarmuid and the scribes were among the first to depart and as the Vikings approached the monastery they were already in the leather boat. They hoped that Declan would come across the island later. They had orders to cast off if he did not appear.

'Everything prepared, Brother Declan?' Connachtach asked.

'As prepared as it could be.'

'Your plan may perhaps save many of our members. Perhaps you were right about monasteries. They are built in the wrong places and should be defended with walls.'

'And also by towers. If I had a man on a watch tower I would know exactly when these mongrels were approaching.'

As Declan looked towards the sea, he saw a large square sail emerge, with its hideous sea serpent. Then he saw the ship itself, much larger than he had expected and standing at the back above the marauders in the belly of the ship, Sigmund the Red, the largest man he had ever seen, perhaps of equal stature with himself.

'Prepare the tallow candles,' he called to the monks standing behind the high wall. Throw them when I give the signal. They must be all thrown together. We must have an even fire. And keep away from the pits.'

They waited in silence for the order.

SIGMUND THE RED WONDERED what lay behind the wall set up before the monastery. He could not see any activity beyond the barricade. Perhaps the monastery was empty. He ordered the anchor to be dropped and the rope sails loosened. The men stood at the ready.

'Over the side and shorewards,' he ordered. 'Let gold be the prize.'

Men jumped over the sides of the ship into the sea in ordered sequence. As they waded ashore Declan lowered his arm. Immediately the monks threw the tallow candles onto the high bank. With leather hides they fanned the flames which crackled through the whins. Smoke rose up from the wall and was carried seawards towards the ship. The monks grabbed their scythes and stood at either side of the entrance.

The crew were almost ashore when Sigmund saw the smoke and flames. He had been tricked. He wished to call his men back but the battle urge was upon them and the brittle sound of the fire was louder than his voice. His men were taken by surprise. The bank was a huge furnace.

The Vikings rushed through the five entrances hoping to get quickly through the searing heat. They cried out their fearful battle cries. Their cries were soon turned to cries of agony. As they rushed through the gaps, the man traps gave way and many of them were impaled upon the menacing points. Others tripped upon them and also fell into the pits.

'Use the scythes. Use the scythes. Don't give them a chance to recover. Every Viking dead is a monk saved,' Declan called. He rushed to a pit, his sword humming about him, men open–mouthed at his strength and his agility with the huge sword. Screaming he bore down upon the trapped men, hacking and killing in battle frenzy. His battle cry put ferocity into the hearts of the monks. They cut at the Vikings as they rushed through the gaps, over the forms of their fallen companions.

Sigmund watched his own men back away from the entrances. He quickly jumped over the side of his ship, drew his sword and waded swiftly ashore. 'What in the name of Thor has happened?' he called to one of his men dragging himself wounded towards the boat.

'They had set animal traps beyond the entrance. Half the crew are dead. Call a retreat.'

'There will be no retreat. I will not let it be known in the fjords of Norway that I was tricked by soft monks.'

Sigmund, had he been wise, would have called a retreat. He gathered his men and ordered them forwards. Some of

The assault on the monastery

them got through on the second attempt, climbing over the impaled bodies of their dead comrades.

'Thor defend me.' Sigmund called out. 'Send your thunder from the skies and your ravens to pick the bones of my enemies.'

He passed over the bodies of his dead men and rushed into the compound. He gazed about him in blazing anger and then he saw Declan. He looked strange in his monk's robe, his bald head, the old wound mark running from forehead to chin. There was battle anger in his eyes. Sigmund saw him kill two of his men, with fast direct strokes. 'So this is the soldier monk,' he thought.

'Soldier monk.' He called in his Nordic tongue. 'Face the one who will feed you to Thor's ravens.'

The two giant men approached each other, eye locked to eye, swords in front, pointing downwards. They circled preparing to do battle. Their swords clashed. They felt the shock run through their bodies. Declan, more adept, drew quickly back with his sword, and with left and right strokes, bore down upon the Viking, who parried awkwardly, beating off the blows.

'Now Viking dog, you know what it is to fight an equal fight. Monk killer and destroyer of monasteries,' Declan roared.

Battle ceased about them and men looked at the greatest single handed battle that would take place in the eighth century. It would be recorded in Irish and Nordic legend.

Declan knew from the beginning that Sigmund was an awkward swordsman and too slow witted for his nimble mind. So while he battled with him, he planned the steps he would take. Perhaps he could save many of the surviving monks. He knew that if he killed Sigmund, his plans might be foiled. The fire was now dying behind them and they could see the Viking ship and the sea. The entrances in the fire wall were littered with dead.

Declan's eyes were about him. An enemy might approach from the back. One did. With several quick blows to left and to right he knocked Sigmund off his balance, then swept quickly around and in one circular sweep cut off the raised sword arm, and was immediately facing Sigmund again. He must ease his pace he thought and let Sigmund use up some of his strength. He backed towards one of the entrances and Sigmund feeling that the tide of victory might be flowing in his direction attacked ferociously. Each stroke slid down Declan's sword handle. He backed further towards the entrance and Sigmund rushed him roaring and hacking until he was out of breath. Then with a sudden move, Declan was behind him and Sigmund had his back towards the entrance. Declan then bore down upon Sigmund with such a rapidity of strokes that he did not know from what direction they came. The sword became a menacing shield, whirring this way and that. Sigmund backed throught the entrance, slipped on the blood and as he was falling Declan whipped his sword from his hand and sent it spinning in an arc towards the sea. Declan had his arm about him, a dagger at his throat.

'Tell these mongrels, Canneck' he cried to a young monk who spoke the Nordic tongue, 'that if they move I will slit the throat of their leader.'

He dragged Sigmund to his feet and holding the dagger to his throat, moved backwards towards the sea.

'And now Canneck, get two tallow candles and set the ship on fire. That will give them something to occupy their minds! Those monks who can make the sound hail the boats from the mainland. You have still a chance to escape.'

'Shall we carry the remains of Connachtach with us?' one asked.

'No, you will later be able to return for your dead.'

The monks quickly rushed from the place of battle towards the shore opposite the mainland. Declan watched them depart. Declan knew that Sigmund was scheming in his mind.

'He will not kill me, men,' he called,' I feel the battle urge leaving his body. He is becoming a monk again.'

The Vikings broke rank and moved forwards. The battle savagery returned to Declan. He cut a gash in Sigmund's face. Sigmund screamed in pain. He had never been marked on the face before.

'Enda,' he called a young monk who remained, 'climb aboard the ship and throw out four sets of oars.' Enda did as he was ordered. The tide took them seawards.

The Vikings watched each move. They watched Canneck move towards the ship with two tallow candles.

'Do not move until I tell you, Canneck.'

Down along the coast the monks were moving across the sound in small boats. Fortune was in their favour.

'Now burn the ship,' he ordered. Enda jumped overboard and Canneck threw the lighted candle on the sail. It began to burn, then it began to blaze: Declan's eyes were on many things and his concentration weakened. With a quick snap Sigmund turned, whipped out his dagger and slashed Declan on the arm. He would have plunged it in his chest but he saw the smoke rising from his ship.

'Save the ship,' he roared, 'or we shall never sail again.' He rushed towards his ship. 'I shall meet with you again, monk,' Sigmund called. 'We have a final battle to fight.'

Declan called on Canneck and Enda to follow him. He fled across the island to the cove where Sixtus awaited him. He climbed aboard and Sixtus hoisted the sail.

Declan had lost a lot of blood. A great tiredness crept over his body and lying on the floor of the boat, he slipped into a deep sleep as he always did after the ferocity of battle. He had made one mistake. He should have destroyed the ship.

The mist had cleared over the island during the battle. It did not suit Sixtus. He would have to change his plans. He would have to hold to the coast and sail between dangerous rocks. His journey would not be as direct as he had expected. Many of the dangerous journeys would have to be made at night.

The leather boat, carrying double sail, set a course eastwards from the island. It carried twelve men, the great book and its golden cover.

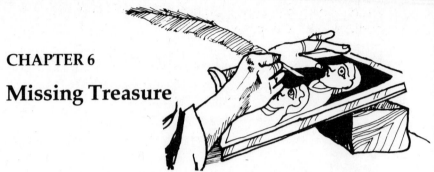

CHAPTER 6

Missing Treasure

SIGMUND THE RED, having wounded Declan rushed to his blazing ship. The silks had caught fire and the hold was burning. The other crew members waded through the water, sometimes falling forward into the waves, in their eagerness to save the ship.

'Cut the sail ropes,' Sigmund ordered, 'and get the sail and yard into the sea.' Working feverishly depite the heat, they pushed the yard and the sail over the side and the waiting Vikings pulled it away from the ship. They spread the sail out in the water and examined the damage. The central part, carrying the Sea Serpent, had been burned.

'Has the fire burned the timbers?' Sigmund roared up from the sea.

'No' cried one of his men. 'They are only blackened.'

He climbed on board to investigate. The mast was scorched, the central timbers charred. He scraped them with his sword. The burns were not deep.

'Torgein,' he called to a Viking youth. 'I am going ashore. Scour the black scores from the ship. It offends my eye.'

Sigmund's crew, having quenched the flames, sat at the ends of the ship, confused and silent. It was beyond their thoughts that they had been so easily trapped. The monks, they had been told, were men of God, yet they had savaged their companions with scythes. But above all they thought of Declan, the soldier monk. Rolv had been correct. They had never seen one so nimble on his feet, so fast with his sword. In single combat he would have killed them all. To him Sigmund the Red owed his life.

'He must have been possessed by an evil spirit. His sword moved so quickly that it was in many places at once. The monk's god must be stronger than Thor,' someone said.

'He is more than man, that monk. He is perhaps half god and is now back in the halls of the gods reclining after battle,' another added.

'Snivelling, whinging cowards,' Sigmund roared. 'He is no god. He bleeds. Did I not turn upon him and plunge my dagger in his arm? At this moment he is probably somewhere on the island dying. Had I not slipped on the very blood of my men, the fight would have gone a different way.'

'We have never seen a greater fighter,' one was bold enough to say.

'Fools,' roared Sigmund. 'Had you waited my orders to attack, you would not have been destroyed. I saw the trap. Hasten. We have our dead to bury.'

Reluctantly they slipped overboard, into the sea and waded ashore. They buried their dead in the pits, heaping a mound of earth over each trap. Then they went from cell to cell in search of gold, only to discover simple furnishings and rough bedding. In the guest house they discovered the body of the sailor from Roland Dirk's ship.

'They have taken everything,' they told Sigmund. 'Nothing of worth remains.'

'There must be gold somewhere. The ornaments of Iona are famous. Their chalices are so large that a man could fill them with a barrel of wine. I tell you there is gold not far from where we stand.'

While he talked with some of his men, a Viking rushed up and said that they had discovered a monk alive.

'Drag him here,' Sigmund said. 'If he knows where the gold is I will soon unlock his tongue. Start a fire.' The monk Patrick had been knocked unconscious during the battle. Still confused he was dragged into the presence of Sigmund, whose very appearance terrified him.

'Where is the monastery treasure?' Sigmund asked.

'I cannot tell. I cannot tell.' Patrick said.

'Then I shall be forced to burn all the buildings. Your friends are tied and bound within the church.'

Patrick looked at the buildings. His fellow brothers would suffer a terrible death.

'If you do not talk, your friends will fry.'

Patrick hesitated for a moment. Then he spoke. 'The ornaments on our book cover are our great treasures. They are on their way to Ireland.'

'Who carries them?'

'Sixtus.'

'When did he depart?'

'Perhaps three hours ago.'

Sigmund the Red looked at the cringing monk. He would have killed him as easily as he would have swatted a fly.

'Get out of my sight!' Sigmund roared. 'I am sick of praying monks. Go and tell Declan that Sigmund the Red will meet him someday in an even battle. Run!'

With that, Patrick, still confused about what was happening, rushed from the compound.

Sigmund the Red wished to be alone. He walked out through the entrance of the enclosure and up the hill. He sat where Columcille had often sat when he looked southwards towards Ireland. Sigmund would have wept bitter tears had he not been trained in his youth to look upon tears as a sign of weakness in a man. The monk Declan had blemished the most beautiful ship ever built in the fjords. A patched ship was not a ship at all. Many of the oars, lovingly whittled during the long winter evening in his house, were now floating on every tide, and the sail, stitched under the supervision of his wife Asta, would carry a grey patch. It was fit only for a barn cover. Rolv of Shetland would laugh when he heard the story. The glory which he had sought, the gold with which he would build a fleet of ships, and the final great moment of his existance, burial with his ship, seemed now outside his grasp. Rolv of

Shetland would place a price upon his head and scour the seas for the one who betrayed a trust.

There was only one course to follow. He would track down this monk for one final single-handed battle. He must destroy the beautiful book – the most beautiful book in the world, it was said. A monk had destroyed his ship. He would destroy the book. They would be even.

He wondered how Sixtus might sail for Ireland. He knew the Viking mastery of the sea so he would not take a direct course. He would move along the headlands and among the islands and either sail at night time from the Mull of Kintyre or the Mull of Galloway. Given the fact that he carried the most beautiful book in the world as cargo, and its ornamented cover, he would be extra cautious. Sigmund would follow him.

He looked at the island. He wondered why these monks should have come to so bleak a place to build their monastery. They worshipped a strange god, a god of peace, but no god was equal to Thor. He made his way down the hill and back into the enclosure. It was as silent as the halls of the dead. He looked at the fresh clay heaped over his men and remembered the trap into which he had been so easily led.

His crewmen had almost patched the sail. The ugly patch, awkwardly stitched, offended his eye. 'Shall we sail today, Sigmund?' one of the crew asked.

'Not before we drink to the memory of our comrades. Break open the monastery wine.' Taking his sword, he broke off the earthen necks and handed the wine to his men. He drank deeply of the red wine. His men followed. Soon they would be drunk.

'To the dead,' he cried. 'May they sup tonight with our gods in Valhalla.'

'To the dead,' they answered.

'Sigmund has resolved to share all his gold equally among his crew members.' He told them.

'No sea captain has ever been so generous,' they replied.

It had never been known before that a sea captain had divided his spoils equally among his men. If they could capture another treasure ship, then they would return to their fjords as rich men and all the humiliation would be forgotten. Sigmund knew that such an offer would bring the crewmen with him and quell rebellion.

Later they brought the patched sail aboard, and hoisted it. They put the remaining oars in the oar-ports and, with drunken strokes, rowed away from the shore. They could see the dark track of whin ash running along the sand and the five mounds which marked the resting place of their comrades. Beyond the ashen mark lay the monastery compound, the buildings of wattle and straw still intact, the bodies of the unburied monks lying in the open spaces.

Sigmund looked at the sail now filled with wind. It was patched and ugly. It carried them out to sea and then southwards. The hunt for Declan the soldier monk and the great book and its precious cover was on.

CHAPTER 7

The Island of Flowers

DECLAN SLEPT DEEPLY as Sixtus brought them down the coast. Sixtus knew that they could not outsail the Viking. While Declan slept, the Coptic monk, Brother Sergius, bandaged the wounded arm. They would have to put in at some small monastery and permit him to rest. Brother Enda explained what happened on the beach.

'Never in my life have I seen so much confusion. I stood at the barricade, trembling, waiting for the invader to come and knowing that my life was in great danger. I thought I would not live through the day.'

'They never suspected that we had laid a trap for them,' Canneck added.

'And what of Declan?' Ciarán asked.

'He had the battle frenzy on him, just like we heard in the story. As if some spirit was in possession of his body. And to see the movement of his sword. It was miraculous.'

'And Connachtach died,' Diarmuid added.

'Yes. He could have lived had he left with the others. I heard him call out the name of Columcille as he died.'

The great book was now in Diarmuid's care. It was safely wrapped in sheepskin, set in the hull and well protected from the sea. He looked at the great artist Paul, so short sighted that he had no idea where he was. About him were grey images.

'It is a world of ghosts, Diarmuid, this world about me,' he had often said. 'It is only when I bend towards the book that I see clearly. I have given my vision to the book.'

The Coptic monk, with his wide brow and burnished skin, who spoke very little, sat beside the figure of Declan.

'You must search out a monastery or village, Sixtus,' he said. 'Declan needs herbs and food. He continues to lose blood.'

Sixtus moved along the southern coast of Mull. He listened to the sound of the waves rushing up on the shore and the sound of the sea ahead of him. The wind was carrying the boat along too quickly. A wrong decision on his part and the leather would be sliced by a sharp rock.

'Diarmuid,' he called. 'Gather in the main sail.' He waited for the mist to close around them from the south. Then he ordered Diarmuid to hoist the sail again. He swung the boat about, and set his course away from the coast. The mist would protect them. It was a fine mist, which penetrated his habit. It did not unduly disturb him. The wind would blow it dry again.

He held his course and listened to the sea. It had many voices. Soon he would be passing the island of Luing. Then they would be safely among the small islands leading to the South of Jura. Beyond that was the island of Scarba.

'We are fortunate that you know the seas so well. You sail in dangerous places with great confidence.' Enda said.

'I know all the movements of the great waters. I tried once to live in a small cell by a lake but the quietness roared in my head and I could not sleep at night. There is seal flesh in the calf of my leg. Once a sea monster attacked our boat and bit off part of my calf. An old monk killed a seal, and, with the blood still warm, placed part of its back to my leg. It grafted well, so part of me belongs to the strange depths of the sea and I have a knowledge of all that is happening beneath us.'

'How far have you sailed, Sixtus?' Canneck asked.

'Further than Brendan. Beyond the verges of the world. I have sailed through a sea of kelp and I have walked on beaches of golden sands and ate strange fruit and food.'

'It should be written down in the books. It is a story of

great wonder,' Canneck told him.

'And so it is. But I would prefer to forget it. I brought young men on a reckless voyage and they all died. I had to bury them at sea. So I have no wish to recall the monstrous things which happened.'

He knew that they were listening to his story. It would help them forget the dangerous seas through which they were now passing. They came out of the mist. They were moving through many islands. Sixtus had brought them across the Firth of Larne. They were amazed at the exactness of their position in the channel between the islands.

'It is impossible that one should have such a knowledge of the sea,' the Coptic monk said as he looked about him with his strange luminous eyes.

'Not impossible, brother, when you know the sounds of the waves on the different shores.'

'Do you think we shall find a place to hide and rest from the Vikings? Declan continues to loose blood.'

'I shall bring him to the island called Paradise. There Iarla will take care of him. We should not intrude upon his quiet life and that of his monks for they spend their days in contemplation.'

'Does he not fear the Vikings?'

'Why should he fear the Vikings on his island of Paradise? Vikings do not come to pick flowers. Their desires are set only on gold.'

They moved to the south of the island of Scarba. They looked shorewards. They could only see low cliffs and sinister rocks. As Sixtus moved towards the rocks, the monks thought they would surely tear the boat with their ragged teeth. Sixtus lined his boat with a mark on the cliff. A swell caught them and they shot forward on a high wave between the rocks. They found themselves in a quiet bay. Unseen from the sea, there was an open arch of rock at the base of the cliff. 'Take down the sails,' he commanded. 'We will row through the opening.'

In quiet wonder, they passed beneath the arch. It was

barely large enough to take the boat. Working their hands on the vault above them, they inched forwards until they were in a quiet bay, surrounded by a beautiful valley.

'You have come through the gates of Paradise,' Sixtus said. But they did not hear his words. Already their lungs were full of luxurious, sleep–inducing perfumes carried across the bay on quiet winds. They had never seen so many flowers before, so well blended and set out on a pattern on the hill. And the pattern was made firm by small pathways through the flowers and shrubs. As soon as Diarmuid looked at the valley he knew that he had seen this pattern of colours somewhere before.

'It's the Chi Rho page from the great book,' he marvelled.

'I know,' said Sixtus. 'I drew it for Iarla a long time ago when Brother Paul set about designing it. As the page grew so did the colours. Many of the inks used in the book come from this island.'

Sixtus let the boat drift towards the small stone pier. Iarla was waiting for them with three of his monks. Diarmuid noticed that their skins were as fine as milk, without a wrinkle, and they moved to a quiet rhythm.

'My friend Sixtus, harvester of the sea, you must have brought your friends here for a very good reason.'

'I throw myself upon your charity, Iarla. Indeed I am sorry to break the secret of your valley, known only to Connachtach and I, but we have had strange adventures and one of our monks is ill.'

'And how is Connachtach?' Iarla asked.

'He has been killed by Viking raiders.'

'I am sad to hear such news. He came to me as a young boy, you know. Ah well. He wished to go to Iona. But come quickly ashore. We shall talk later.'

The monks, cramped after their journey in the uncomfortable boat, climbed on to the pier. The island monks lifted the heavy body of Declan from the boat. The abbot ordered them to bring him to the infirmary.

'And who is this young monk, Sixtus?' Iarla asked.

'This is the young scribe Diarmuid. I do not boast when I say that he is the most skilled of all who work in the scriptoria. Even at a young age he had mastered his craft.'

'He has worked on the great book, then?'

'He is now master of the great book. You once prayed that in a vision you might behold the great book of which I have often spoken.'

'I have often thus prayed, but they were foolish requests.'

'Your request has been granted. We carry the great book itself in the boat. Connachtach ordered us to flee the island. Tonight Diarmuid will show you all the glorious pages and the dogs and cats and otters I have often spoken about.'

They began to move up through the paths, Diarmuid and Enda carrying the satchels between them.

'Sixtus,' Diarmuid asked, 'how could Iarla know Connachtach as a young man?'

'You remember the story of the land of eternal youth?

'Yes, I do.'

'Well, Iarla is over one hundred years of age. Some say that he is over one hundred and twenty and can remember the early saints. He knows the secrets of nature so well and the healing which is in every plant and he knows the secret of prolonging youth.'

'Then why does he not let the whole world know of it?'

'Because the world would not use such secrets well.

'It is truly paradise.'

'In all the world there is no wonder like this and when Iarla dies it will return again to the wilderness from which it sprang. No animal is killed here. The monks live on vegetables and herbs which they cultivate themselves.

'He has many plants here which I have never seen before.

'Iarla travelled the known world looking for them and brought them back as seedlings.'

'We could finish the book here, Sixtus,' he suggested.

'No. We would not. We would loose interest. You would become a gardener. Connachtach ordered me to take the book to Ireland and that order binds me like chains.

The Island of Flowers

They moved up through the gardens. The path turned in
many directions among flowers which Diarmuid had never
seen before. Each flower had a different scent. Sometimes
they passed a garden filled with herbs, at another time they
stopped and looked at waterfalls pouring down into stone
pools.

'It is never–ending, Sixtus.'

'True. The paths are so arranged that you never have to
pass over the same one during a day's walk.'

They finally reached the monastery proper. The church
was built from thin slabs of stone, the roof of blue slate.
About the church stood the small stone cells. In a small
garden close to a waterfall stood the infirmary. It was a
spacious place and Declan was placed on a pallet of heather.
He regained consciousness after some time and he looked
about in wonder.

'You are in good hands,' Diarmuid told him. 'You have
saved many lives today. But now you must place yourself
under the care of abbot Iarla.'

Iarla ordered his monks to bring Declan a drink. 'You will
sleep very deeply after this,' Iarla told him holding the vessel
to his lips. 'When you are asleep I can attend your wound.'

After Declan had taken the honeyed drink, he fell into a
deep sleep. Iarla cut away his sleeve and looked at the deep
wound. Gently he cleaned away the blood and poured
stinging liquid into the gash. Then he closed the wound
and did a strange thing. He threaded a needle and stitched
the wound and then placed ointment over it.

'It will bind during the night and all that will be left in a
few days is a slight mark. He will sleep deeply. Tomorrow
I shall give him herbs which cure from within.'

They left the infirmary and went to the refectory. They
ate the vegetables set before them and drank the honey. It
was almost dark now over the valley. The monks brought
candles to the refectory and Diarmuid showed them the
great book. They looked at each page with reverence, not
daring to touch it. It was very late when they quenched the

candles and made their way to their cells. The island monks, full of wonder, had seen the great book. The monks of Iona, also full of wonder, had seen the valley. Quickly they fell asleep, breathing the perfumes of the garden.

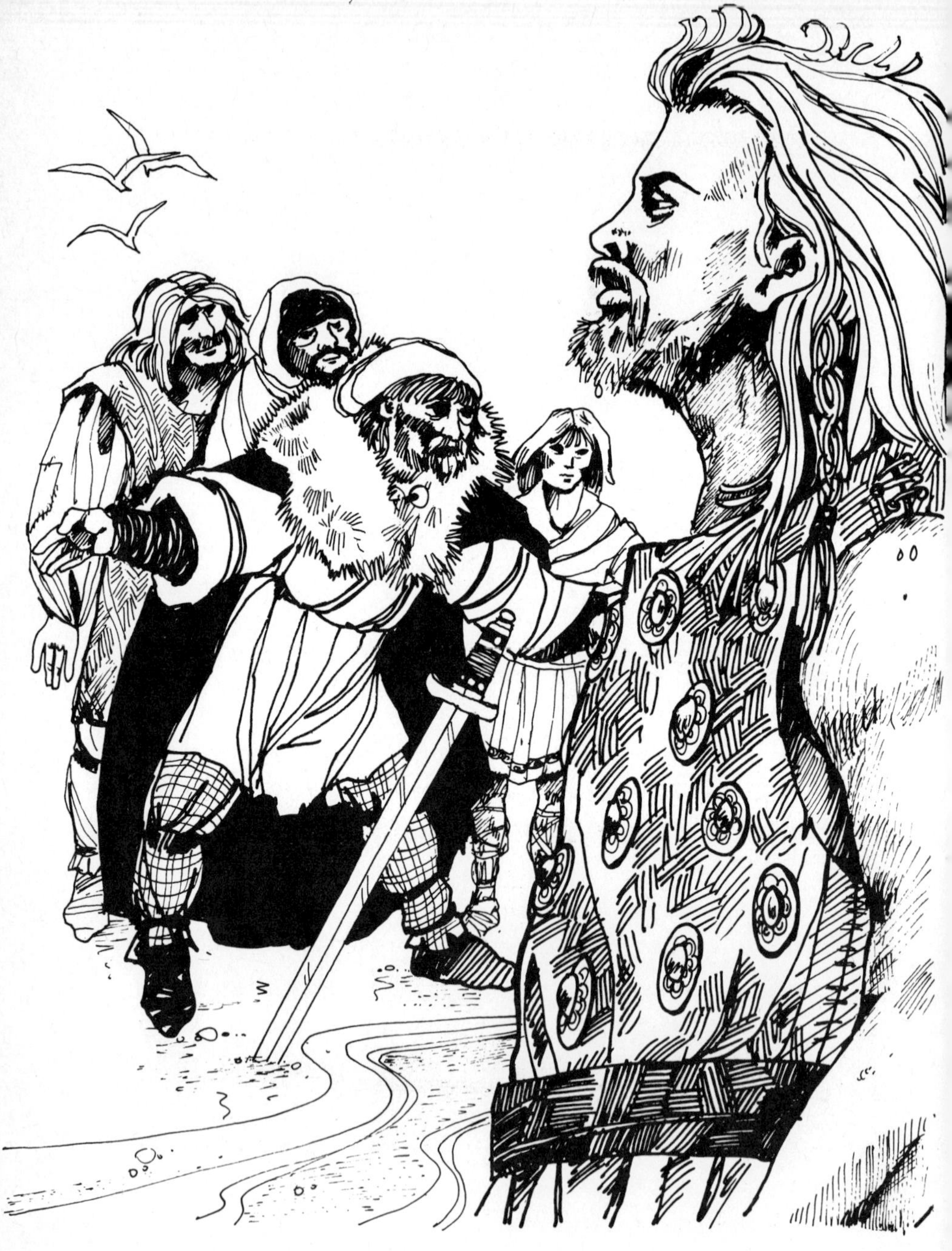

CHAPTER 8

Rolv's Laughter

'ONE OF US MUST DIE.' Sigmund the Red muttered to himself as he looked at his patched sail and smelt the charred wood. The soldier monk had maimed his ship. Only half his crew remained. They were dispirited and drunk.

He followed the southern coast of Mull. At evening he noticed a fishing village set in a small bay. They would have noticed a boat passing down the strait. If he sailed directly into the bay, the villagers might take flight. He decided, instead, to take some gold and swim ashore. 'If I do not return in one hour, come in search of me,' he told his men.

He removed his heavy jerkin and helmet. Then he stood on the side of his ship and dived into the sea. With firm strokes he swam towards the shore. He had been observed by the men of the village.

'Why does he come alone?' They asked each other. 'He is exposing himself to danger.'

'We will soon discover his purpose. Have your swords ready,' the village chief warned.

Sigmund waded ashore, unbuckled his sword and threw it on the sand.

'Fetch the sword,' the village leader directed. A young man ran forward and collected the heavy sword. They were surprised at the huge size of the Viking, with his red beard and long red hair.

Sigmund took two gold coins and threw them on the

sand. They dashed forward and fought for them on the strand.

He knelt down and with his dagger, drew the outline of a leather boat and sail. They understood. One came forward and drew a second sail on the boat. Sigmund was surprised at this. The sailor monk had a boat with two sails which meant that he would handle the craft with great skill and accuracy.

He then walked the beach until they told him to stop. He now knew the length of the boat. He determined to discover more. He took a stone and placed it on the sand, then he drew a boat and pointed to his ship. They understood that the stone represented the island. Quickly they gathered other stones, burying some in the sand to indicate reefs. Very soon he had a pattern of the sea and the island. One marking he could not understand. Beside one island they had placed flowers. They drank in deep breaths as if to indicate a delicious scent.

'I'm not here to pick flowers,' he told them in a language they did not understand. 'I am here in search of an enemy and to settle an old score.'

It was clear to Sigmund that the sailor monk was making his way through treacherous reefs. He would not follow him. He would catch him as he made his way down between Jura and Kintyre. He would slaughter the crew, take the book cover and tear the great book page by page and consign the fragments to the vagaries of every tide. He threw some coins far beyond them and while they scrambled after them, he took his sword and returned to his ship.

'We shall capture them in the Straits of Jura,' he told his crew. 'I shall have my revenge. Then we will return to the fjords and build a fleet of ships.'

Further up the coast he found a secluded bay. They anchored for the night and pitched their camp. The crewmen's camps were some distance from Sigmund's and when they spoke it was in whispers. They were sober now.

'It is time to return to the fjords. We have gold and silk from the treasure ship. We will be rich men if Sigmund divides the spoils fairly,' Harald of Grotli whispered.

'Divide the spoils? Sigmund is tight fisted. He will not divide the spoils. We sail an unlucky ship,' his friend Einar said.

'We had good luck in the beginning, but now it has turned against us. Rolv of Shetland will be in our wake. We do a dangerous thing, following this soldier monk. Never have I seen such sword play in my life,' Harald continued.

'Sigmund cannot return to the fjords. The story of our defeat will spread rapidly over the land. We would be the butt of ridicule in all the villages,' Einar told him.

'The anger in Sigmund's mind blinds him to caution. All his life he dreamed of building a beautiful ship which would be faster and larger than any which sailed. In one morning she was almost destroyed. Her timbers are scorched, her proud emblem maimed,' Harald continued, his voice low.

'I understand that. That is why we must plan for our own safety. With Sigmund dead we could sail directly home. With Sigmund alive we could sail these seas forever in search of the soldier monk. We must consider our own safety,' Einar advised.

Sigmund sat in a hunched position over his fire. 'I will follow him to the very edge of the world,' he thought. 'Next time we will fight in my own element, the sea.' He watched the fire burn out. Then he entered his tent, wrapped his cloak about him and fell asleep. His dreams were troubled by many images.

ON THE ISLAND OF SCARBA Declan slept a day and a night. His strength returned. The scent of flowers was everywhere. The music of the birds and the waterfalls came up from the valley.

'His arm will only carry a thin mark. If the wound parts, I will give you an ointment to pour into it,' Iarla told Diarmuid.

'Will Declan be troubled again by the visions of battle?' Diarmuid asked.

'That I cannot tell you. At the moment he is untroubled but the images may return again.'

'We will not disturb him,' Iarla said, and they left the infirmary.

While they were talking, Sixtus made his way up through the paths to the rim of the valley. He continued to walk across the back of the island. To the north would be Iona and to the west the island of Colonsay. As he looked towards Iona his eye caught the sight of a Viking ship passing Eileach an Naoimh. He threw himself on the ground and peering between two boulders looked at the ship. He marvelled at the movement of the ship and her graceful lines. His leather boat, good for shallows and awkward places along the coast, could not move at great speed upon the sea. This ship would bear down upon him like a swift hound.

He moved down behind a hill and passed across the island towards Corrievrechan whirlpool. Away from the perfume of the valley and looking down on the vast whirling mass of water, with its sinister empty mouth, ready to drag an unsuspecting boat down to the depths of the sea, he could make his plans. He wondered what the Viking was thinking of that very moment. He probably suspected that they were among the islands and he would try and block them somewhere in the Sound of Jura. They could no longer stay at the island of Scarba and Sixtus could not see his way out of the trap which Sigmund might set for him. He listened to the noise of the whirlpool beneath him. Its waters boiled and tangled about the dark eye. He had studied its moods many times in the past. It was more like a sea monster than a whirlpool and it had a life of its own. It had an insatiable craw and it guarded the passage between Scarba and Jura. As he looked at the empty socket of water beneath him, a desperate plan entered his mind. He thought about it for an hour. Satisfied that it might be possible, he made his way back across the island. They could afford to spend another night with Iarla.

WHILE SIGMUND THE RED was preparing to attack Iona, Ragnvald, Rolv's sea captain, hastened back to the Shetlands, with a firm following wind. Rolv was surprised to see his captain return. He knew instantly that something was wrong. During the years he had built up his fleet of ships. He offered the southern traders and the monks protection from invaders if they paid the danegeld. His trading and the protection he offered brought him a constant flow of gold.

As he watched Ragnvald's ship enter the harbour he was worried. He returned to the long house and waited for his sea captain. He drank a horn of wine and thought of

Sigmund the Red.

'Where is the southern ship?' He asked in a sullen mood when Ragnvald entered.

'There is no southern ship. We discovered a burnt out hulk when we reached the island. All the crewmen had been slain.'

'Only one man could have done such a deed and that villain is Sigmund the Red.' Rolv roared in anger banging his wine hand on the table.

'We did find a Viking dagger on the beach. The markings show the locality of the attackers.' He placed the dagger on the table. Rolv examined the markings on the handle.

'I do not need this evidence to tell me who it was. This Sigmund and his crewmen move like a dangerous pack of wolves through the sea. Well he knows that Rolv protects the trading ships and the monasteries. Word of this will reach the harbours of the south. We shall not be trusted anymore. We must hunt him down.'

'I told our ship to stand by at Rhum and watch the seas. I sent word to our other ship at the island of Harris to sweep south.'

'You did well. We must all move against him. I will destroy his ship. He will not have the pleasure of sailing to Valhalla in it. Have stores brought to the ships. It will take us three days to reach Rhum. I will take charge of the ships. I weary of island life.'

Ragnvald left the great hall. He ordered his crewmen ashore to eat and rest. Food was placed before them. Then they lay in the boxed beds lined with clean straw and fell asleep. Rolv, his anger now controlled, went to his house. His wife Astrid was waiting for him. She was of royal blood and Rolv trusted her more than any other person in the world.

'My husband is worried,' she said when she saw him enter.

'Your husband is a fool, Astrid. In this very village I betrayed Roland Dirk in drink. Wine is not good for man.

Sigmund pretended to sleep but his ears were open.

'He is a fox, this Sigmund,' Astrid said.

'No. He is a wolf. But I will track him across the oceans, Astrid.'

'You are no longer young, Rolv. Life on the island has perhaps taken the edge for battle off you.'

'You speak too honestly, Astrid. Indeed, I sometimes feel ague in my body. This will be my last sea chase. Until the seas are cleared of these sea wolves, no trading ship will venture into these waters. I will sleep a little now. Polish my sword, my helmet and my shield. I will set out this very night.'

'Sleep. I will close the door of the room and there will be no noise about the house.' She closed the door of the small room and went in search of his armour.

That evening he buckled on his jerkin which had rested in a wooden chest for two years. He belted on his sword and fitted his helmet on his head. He felt the desire for the sea and the sea chase.

'The gods of war be on your side and may the winds fill your sails,' Astrid said as he left the house.

He gathered his men about him in the long house. They were surprised at his appearance. He looked like a warrior from the past. He took a horn of wine and lifted it in a toast.

'To the sea chase!' He called.

'To the sea chase!' They all called in return.

'Let us now move towards the ships,' he ordered when the horns were empty. It was late evening now and a good breeze blew seawards. They went aboard, raised their sails and moved out of the harbour. It would take them a night and a day of sailing to reach the North Minch. At Little Minch they would join Rolv's third ship and the fourth would join them off the island of Rhum. Rolv steered the ship directly west and late that night he handed the tiller over to one of his men and went to sleep among his crew.

Dawn came slowly out of the grey east. There was no land in sight. The crew brushed the sleep from their eyes and ate their morning meal which consisted of bread and cheese washed down with milk. They then manned the oars and rowed at an even pace for three hours. By evening they were joined by the first ship. That night they sailed towards Rhum, each within lantern distance of one another. They would seek out Iona and see perhaps if the monks had some knowledge of Sigmund.

THE MONKS RETURNED to Iona the day after Sigmund's departure. They came in small groups and made their way into the enclosure. They were surprised that so little damage had been done. They spent the day burying the monks who had died in battle.

When they visited the scriptorium, and looked at the torn satchels and scattered pages of vellum they knew that the great days of the monastery were over. There would never again be an abbot like Connachtach who would gather so many great artists about him and undertake a work as difficult as that of the great book.

Some days later they saw four Viking ships on the horizon. Their menacing sails grew larger and larger. They looked at the markings which the ships carried and knew that Rolv of Shetland had arrived. From the sea it appeared that the monastery had been unmolested but as Rolv reached the shore it was apparent that something had recently happened. There were strange mounds of earth close to the shore and he wondered what had caused the black mark which ran between the mounds.

'I come in peace,' he called to the monks. 'My men wait on the ships. I do not come for the danegeld but for news of a red Viking wolf who has slipped into these waters.'

'He has come and he has departed.' one of the monks told him.

'Then he has left little trace of his visit.'

'He has, Rolv. The mounds of earth you see carry the bodies of his best warriors.'

'Tell me what has happened.'

'Declan set a trap for Sigmund and his men. They rushed through gaps in the burning walls of furze and fell into animal traps.'

'This Declan is truly a great soldier. I wish I had him on board my ship and leading my men into battle. He would double my wealth and with him guarding my door I could sleep peaceful nights. Never again will Sigmund of the big mouth appear among the warriors gatherings and the wine feasts. In none of the stories is so strange a deed told. Tell me more.' They told him the whole amazing story. Rolv of Shetland began to laugh and when he stopped and thought of what happened, he laughed again.

'Now where is this Declan so great in war that I may bow to him?'

'He has fled the island. He protects the great book.'

'He moves overland then?'

'No, he sails for Ireland under Sixtus the sailor.'

'They are fools to have taken such a course. They will be caught and slaughtered. They should have moved inland.' He was silent for a moment.

'What direction did they take?' he asked.

'We do not know, but two of our monks have seen Sigmund move down the Southern Coast of Mull.'

'The chase is on. Your sailor monk intends to move from headland to headland and then sail directly for Ireland.'

'We do not know, but Sixtus knows the ways of the sea better than any Viking. Once in his leather boat he sailed to the very edge of the world. He never speaks of the strange sights he saw there. He was greyhaired when he returned and all his companions were dead.'

'I will say goodbye now, brothers, and hasten to the sea.' He made his way down the beach stopping now and then to laugh, sometimes bending down and slapping his thighs. He laughed as he waded out to his ship. There were tears of laughter in his eyes when he climbed aboard. He tried to speak and then began to laugh again. Finally between bouts of laughter he told the story to his men. They too began to laugh. Sigmund the Boaster would never face them again. His reputation and his ship had been destroyed by a monk.

Across the water came the sound of laughter, rising and falling on a small wind. The monks looked at each other. Clearly these Vikings were strange beings.

Rolv ordered the oars to be placed in the oar ports. The ships, rising and sinking like slumbering sea creatures, began to move. Rolv must now set a net about Sigmund. If he were to return to the fjords with the treasure he had plundered from Roland Dirk's ship, he could issue from the north the following summer with a fleet. It would destroy Rolv's sea power.

With these thoughts in mind and with his ships well spread out across the sea, Rolv set a course directly south.

for Islay.

CHAPTER 9

The Sea Chase

SIGMUND THE RED had no idea that, as he sailed past the island of Scarba, Sixtus observed his progress. Sixtus knew that he stood no chance against this sleek ship; his journey would have to be at night or through misty weather.

Sigmund was aware of whispers of mutiny among his men. He overheard them say that it was an unlucky ship. The men of his own village doubted his leadership, they would carry the story of his disgrace home to his people. Even the children would mock him. He had to move quickly now for Rolv of Shetland would seek his vengeance.

'We think that you should sail directly home and give up this chase for the monk,' a voice said from among the crew.

'Who dares address me? This ship stinks of mutiny. One mutinous word and you will have to deal with my sword.' Sigmund's voice was hard and threatening.

'I speak for all the crew,' the crewman Kjetil said. 'We have taken council together. We think that this is the only course to follow. Also we fear the vengeance of Rolv.'

'Well, now, fear my vengence!' Sigmund roared. He drew his sword and made to rush among the men. But they drew their swords in answer. A move and he would be a dead man. They would throw him into the sea, take his ship and his gold and disappear.

'Put aside your superstitions. My ship still sails faster than any ship upon the sea. We sail home when we capture the treasure of Iona. Trust Sigmund,'

'How can we trust you? Your treachery is known far and

wide.' Kjetil again spoke.

'At this very moment, I will share the gold we carry among you, if you so wish.'

'We will share it later.'

'Good. It is time to drink more monastery wine. I will send the jars among you. The wind is fair and from the south–west. I will bring the ship between the Island of Islay and Jura. Our approach to the Sound of Jura will not be observed.'

'We will follow the chase for two more days.' Kjetil told him. 'Then, if we do not sight the boat, we shall return home.'

'Agreed, men! Let us seal our agreement in wine.'

One of the crew members passed up the wine jars and they began to drink. Sigmund, standing by the rudder, took a jar of wine and toasted their health and their prosperity. His wine was precious and would have fetched a great price, but he had to dampen their mutiny.

Evening colours filled the sky. The long headlands to the south were becoming dark shapes. Two hours would bring final darkness. Despite the blackened timbers, the ship had not been impaired. He would make his way up through Islay and Jura during the night. Then early in the morning, he would move up through the straits of Jura.

He pressed the lips of the wine jar to his mouth but he did not drink. He pretended that he was as merry as his crew members, and joined in their sea songs. They did not understand the treachery of wine. One by one they fell asleep. When he was satisfied that no one was awake, he moved from the deck and went among them. He would root out the mutiny.

Next morning, when they awoke from their drunken sleep, Kjetil was missing.

They looked up at Sigmund. He was asleep at the tiller. 'He has tricked us,' they whispered. 'You cannot trust Sigmund the fox. This is an unlucky ship. He will lead us to our doom.' Fear ran amongst them. If they rushed at him, he would instantly awake. 'He will not return to our homeland until he kills this strange monk. His hate for him is like poison in his mind and he will not listen to reason.' They ate their bread and cheese slowly, wondering what black evil the day would bring.

Sigmund shook himself from his short sleep. He ordered them to make the oars ready. With the aid of sail and oar, he brought his ship quickly up the Sound of Jura.

THAT NIGHT SIXTUS visited Iarla in his cell: 'We have enjoyed the hospitality of the island. Tomorrow we must sail.'

'Stay one more week and danger will have past. Declan will be well again. If he were to exercise his arm, the wound might open.'

'We must leave, Iarla. At this moment, Sigmund is making his way up the Sound of Jura. He would destroy your valley.'

'But can you escape upon the open sea?'

'Perhaps I can. I have spent many hours looking down upon the whirlpool of Corrievrechan. Here is my plan.'

As Iarla listened to the plan, his face turned ashen. He had never heard anything more reckless in his life: 'In five minutes you could destroy the boat, the monks and the great book itself.'

'I know all these things.. But I have been watching sea-weed floating about the pool. I have watched its every turn as it moved from the edge to the centre. I know the humours and the tides of the whirlpool.'

'It is a spider's web, Sixtus. Anyone who ventures into the narrows will be caught.'

'Better than to suffer death at the hands of the Viking.'

'I know that you are a great sailor, Sixtus. And I know that you have ventured into the unknown, but I think you are rash.'

'I know. Tomorrow at dawn we leave the island.

'My blessings go with you, Sixtus.'

No bell sounded next morning. One of the island monks moved among them and shook them awake. Declan awoke refreshed, his strength now returned.

'Had we such herbs after our battles, then many men would not have died,' he told Iarla.

'Remember that you have a long journey ahead of you. If you tax your arm again, the wound may break open. So I am giving Diarmuid herbs and gut. He will be able to cleanse and stitch the wound.'

Sixtus had arisen before anyone else. He fetched clear water from the well and brought loaves of bread from the monastery bakery. He tested everything on board and then he bailed out the water.

Gradually the monks came down to the stone pier. The Coptic monk was reluctant to leave the island. It reminded him of his home. Scents of flowers which he had forgotten brought back to him the warm luxury of an oasis in the desert. He led Brother Paul by the arm. The world about him was a blur of colour, an illuminated page smudged by mist. The satchels containing the great book and the cover were placed in the hull of the boat.

Before they sailed, Sixtus explained the situation in which they now found themselves, but he did not tell them that they would pass through a treacherous whirlpool.

As they moved out from the hidden bay into the sea, he wondered if his courage exceeded his wisdom. 'Diarmuid,' he asked pointing to the rope and grappling hook. 'Do you think you could cast this among the rocks further down the coast?'

'I think I could.'

'Good. I want Enda and Canneck to man the oars. Follow my instructions exactly.'

They moved down past the island. The tide was beginning to turn. He hoped the Vikings would come when the tide was running at great speed. He looked at the sky and

hoped that it would be a wet misty day. Their safety depended on many things.

Brother Paul was the first to pick up the strange sea sounds.

'What is the whispering I hear?' He asked.

'I can hear no whispering,' the Coptic monk said.

'Listen well. You'll hear the sounds of confused voices.'

The Coptic monk listened attentively: 'Yes! I can hear it now. It is between the islands.'

'It is a whirlpool,' Sixtus announced firmly. 'Our safety lies on the edge of Corrievrechan whirlpool.'

'Corrievrechan! I have heard of it. Such turbulent waters risk death for all.' Enda exclaimed, an edge of fear in his voice.

'Death lies to the west.' Sixtus answered firmly.

They were now a mile from the gulf. They could feel the current's tug beneath the boat. Sixtus steadied the boat and kept his eye to the weather and the tide. Both now suited his purpose.

He steered towards the whirlpool. When he was within two hundred yards of the opening between the islands, he called to Enda and Canneck.

'Keep the boat in position with firm strokes. We are out of the main current at present. Now let us set the bait.'

'What bait?' Diarmuid asked.

'Our boat is the bait. And we are going to catch a large timber fish. Come here, Declan, and with your sound arm hold the tiller firm. Diarmuid and I will hoist the sails when the time is right.'

Five times he went over the instructions until he was certain that each one knew what was expected of him. While he waited he listened to the sound of the whirlpool beckoning to him. Many times he had sailed down the coast and listened to its challenge. This time he had to accept it. There was an urgency in his body. His mind was sea-sharp. This would be his greatest test.

It had begun to rain – a fine mist that reduced visibility.

Suddenly out of the mist, and about a mile away, loomed the menacing Viking ship.

'Shall we hoist the sails, Sixtus?' Diarmuid asked, his voice low but firm.

'The fish has not taken the bait.'

'You are letting him come dangerously near,' Enda warned.

'These are dangerous moments. Obey my orders and do not question my decisions.'

They looked in dread at the great ship. Sigmund the Red had seen them. He was calling to his men. They were preparing for the chase.

'Hoist the sails!' Sixtus called. 'We are on our way. Hold fast to the tiller, Declan, and brace it landwards.'

The orders were obeyed directly. The sails were raised and taken by the wind. The monks rowed into the main current. The leather boat was quickly caught by a mighty force that carried it towards the gap between the islands. Under a firm wind, they passed around the headland where, suddenly, they heard the howling of disturbed waters. Each monk strained forward and soon could see the ever open eye of the whirlpool of Corrievrechan. They knew it could suck them, relentlessly, to the bottom of the sea.

'Hold firmly to the rudder, Declan! Diarmuid! Prepare to cast the grappling hook.' Sixtus roared above the sound of the waters. He watched anxiously as they were carried forward towards the whirlpool that was alive with a hundred quarrelling voices.

Sigmund the Red had moved steadily up the sound since morning, his eye scanning the sea. Somewhere his enemy lurked. His sea sense told him this. He cursed the change in the weather which shortened distance.

And then he saw them, defenceless and close ahead in their small, black leather boat. At the helm, holding the tiller, stood his enemy, Declan. What fools to venture on the sea, his chosen battleground, he thought with satisfaction.

'Drop the sail. Ready the oars and after them,' he roared.

'They cannot escape. The great book cover will be ours. I will take the tiller. Stand beside me, Olaf, and beat the drum!'

Olaf stood beside him and began a slow beat on the drum. The men rowed with an even stroke. The ship sped forward. After stalking the prey for many days, the chase was on. Above the movement of the drum and the even splash of the oars came the distant sound of the still unseen Corrievrechan whirlpool. The Viking ship was now perfectly aligned to course between the two islands. It swept swiftly in from the sea. The undercurrent had already caught it in its force and the crew wondered what sea power was helping them forwards. The gods must surely be on their sides. Now they were three hundred yards from the sea gap between the islands. Again, Sigmund caught a glimpse of the leather boat, with its small sails. It was limping forward and close to the rocks of Jura. The eagle would soon pounce upon the fragile bird and break its back. The rain was blocking his vision.

'Forwards through the straits!' he urged his men. 'We are on direct course. The black boat seems to be floundering on the rocks.'

MEANWHILE, the small leather boat moved carefully. The noise was deafening and as the monks looked at the seething whirlpool, which spiralled downwards towards its dark, empty centre, they were frightened. It was an ugly sea monster's mouth, ready to swallow them down into the craw of the ocean.

'We must hold to the outside currents or we are destroyed,' Sixtus called.

The sails and rudder were doing their work. They were withstanding the inward pull. Uncertain waves at the edge of the whirlpool tossed the boat roughly. They now approached the point where the whirlpool was strongest. The outside circle of water caught them.

'Throw the hook!' he told Diarmuid. Standing in the front of the boat and terrified by the confusion, Diarmuid cast the grappling iron forward. He watched the rope uncurl. It fell among the rocks. He pulled. He could feel the iron fluke tear into the rock. Now the rope was tight in his hands. It was burning his palms, tearing at the soft skin.

'Help, Sixtus, I can hold no longer.'

Sixtus rushed forwards. He looked at the taut rope and hoped the iron grip would hold. If the rope slackened, it would work itself free. They began to haul it in. Hand over hand, they pulled the boat forward out of the current. Slowly the drag lessened and they pulled themselves out from the rim of the whirlpool's power. They were safe. Sixtus had beaten his enemy. He shook the grappling hook free and hauled it back into the boat. The sails and oars carried them forwards. Before them lay the open sea and safety. The monks looked in awe at Sixtus. Only he who once had travelled perilous and unknown seas could have brought them through such dangers in this frail, leather boat.

Too late Sigmund the Red realised that the sailor monk had led him into a trap. The ship, now in mid current, was hurried forwards by the whirlpool. Too late Sigmund became aware of its presence. His ship was firmly in its grip.

He had never known the like in all his travels. It would destroy his ship. The drummer pounded out the oar stroke. Sigmund's gods were failing him. His mind was filled with confusion. Should he plunge on through the whirlpool or pull back from the danger. He called to Olaf to stop the drum beat. It was too late. His men continued to row. Their minds too were filled with confusion. They had never heard such sea noises before. Some broke their rhythm. Their oars tangled. They could not see the eye of the whirlpool, only the confusion of waters boiling about it; the currents were demented, twisting and turning upon one another like eels.

The great ship in trouble

And then the huge ship was taken out of their power. Like a frightened horse it seemed to rise up out of the waters and plunge forward. The oars were wrenched from their hands and they were thrown on their faces. The drummer Olaf, taken by surprise, fell overboard. They watched him carried away and calling for help. His arms thrashed the waters as he was carried about in narrowing circles, until finally he disappeared into the dark empty mouth.

They now realised their full danger. A huge whirlpool had taken control of the ship. They screamed to their gods for help. Sigmund the Red, his arms locked about the dragon prow, was thrown this way and that by the violent movement of the ship. Twice his body was hurled out over the seething waters, to be roughly swung back on board as the ship spun in the waters. His only thoughts were for his safety.

The land swam about them each time the boat, caught by maverick currents within the many tangled spiral, swept them about as they circled. Quickly, Sigmund's seamanship asserted itself. He would have to try and save his ship. He grasped the tiller and pushed it hard from him. The ship steadied on the whirlpool. It circled rapidly, but evenly, about the dark open jaws, no longer tossed or uncontrolled.

'Put out the left oars and pull the ship outwards,' he shouted. The men responded. They took up the loose oars and started to row. Gradually they began to cut the power of the whirlpool, making their way across the currents, towards the outer reaches of the large circle of water.

'We are saved!' They called.

At that moment the keel tore itself on the teeth of a submerged rock. They heard the grating sound beneath the ship. A timber was gashed low in the boat and the sea began to pour in.

Of all the days that Sigmund had sailed the seas, of all the terrible times he had among mountains of floating ice and storm-tossed oceans, this was the worst. The very gods to whom he had dedicated his ship were not on his side. Dazed, he rushed to where his ship was gashed. An ugly tooth of stone showed through the timber. 'Back to the stern!' he ordered. 'Bring all the weight to the stern. Two men lift her off the rocks with the oars.'

They raised the boat from the rocks. It floated back.

'Five men bail the water. The rest row the ship out to sea.'

Dispirited, they rowed the boat seawards away from the whirlpool of Corrievrechan. They now knew that they crewed an unlucky ship.

CHAPTER 10

Tactics

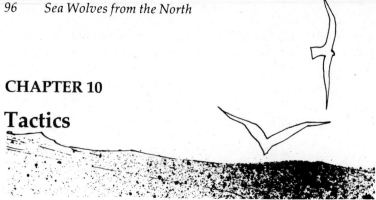

ROLV REACHED COLONSAY. The islanders recognized his ship and as he rowed ashore the men were waiting for him on the beach. He had set up a small trading post there and his ships taken by the uncertain storms which troubled the inner Hebredies could take refuge here.

'Rolv of Shetland, we heard that you were island bound and would never sail the seas again,' the leader said.

'I hunt a mongrel who has crept into my pastures!'

'Two days ago, he sailed between Islay and Jura.'

'And did you see a black leather boat run before him?' Rolv asked.

'You speak of Sixtus the sailor. We have not seen him unless he slipped by at night. You can never be certain of Sixtus. He is a seal.'

He left the islanders a gift of wine and some gold and returned to his ship. He reflected on what moves Sixtus might make. Like Sigmund the Red, he believed that he was lurking in the Sound of Jura. Sixtus had always astonished Rolv. He sailed in black rains, without bearings, in an awkward leather boat. He knew also that Sixtus stood no chance against Sigmund in clear weather. Rolv decided to block off the seas between Islay and Ardminish.

While Rolv ordered his ships to blockade the Sound of Jura, in weather now misty and with limited visibility, Sixtus was chanting a sea prayer to God for having carried him safely through the whirlpool of Corrievrechan.

'A great pity that king David was not a sailor instead of a

shepherd. He would have written sea psalms. Sailors have to compose their own hymns,' he told his fellow monks.

'And poor psalms they are too. They have neither rhyme nor reason,' blind Brother Paul said.

'The Lord listens to the music of our hearts, Brother Paul.'

'And we have to listen to your voice!'

The voice of Sixtus was famous on Iona. He sang in between keys and loudly. 'He was sent to the monastery to torture fine ears,' Paul had complained to Connachtach. 'Leave him be. Leave him be. We must bear with him. He thinks he's as sweet as a thrush in a nut wood,' Connachtach had responded, smiling.

Now Sixtus, in his own element, was singing his sea psalms, as he called them. His heart exulted. He had faced the ultimate challenge. Even Brendan the navigator would not have dared to do what he had just done. He was singing also because the weather suited him. He was hidden for the moment in black rains and he could move down the seas. He prayed for the darkness. Tonight he would make his run for Ireland.

The Coptic monk, wrapped in his double cloak, looked at the dark mysterious sea. Perhaps he would soon be released from all this turmoil and take a ship southwards to his home. To Sixtus he owed his life. He had taken him past the socketless eye of the whirlpool.

'All safe and well?' Sixtus called to the monks.

'All safe and well,' they replied.

'And the satchels?'

'They are dry.'

'We sail directly for Ireland. I pray for winds and storms and black weathers. They are the cover we need. Do not fret about these things, I have been in more dangerous seas. I will eat some bread now if you pass it to me, Diarmuid. Everybody eat.'

The monks looked at each other. They could not eat after

their recent experience.

'I wonder if the Viking has escaped from the whirlpool?' Enda asked.

'Most likely. But he will have got such a bone shaking that he will not forget.'

They sailed as close to the island of Jura as possible, picking up the vagrant winds which carried them along. When the wind did rise, Sixtus moved further out to sea, constantly playing the sails, while Diarmuid held the rudder. That evening they passed Rubha a Mhail at the tip of Islay. Their passage past the point was marked by an islander in the pay of Rolv. They now approached the open sea. Sixtus would now sail for Ireland.

HAVING PASSED THROUGH the demented seas of the whirlpool, Sigmund the Red was still disoriented. His ship was taking water rapidly and his crew members were shaken. They would turn on him if he did not take immediate action. Pulling his sword from his scabbard he rushed among them, hitting them with the flat blade. 'Man the oars!' He roared. 'Bring the ship around the headland. Bail out the water or we shall be drowned. Sigmund has taken you out of danger. You owe your lives to him.'

They were too confused to think. Some took the oars and rowed away from the dark whirlpool, others bailed out the water.

Order gradually returned. Ahead, on the damp misty sea, the monk Sixtus was escaping from Sigmund's clutches in his leather boat, probably laughing at the trap he had set for him. He had now a double score to settle.

'Thor and Odin, send me fine weather and fast winds or abandon me for ever. No prayer I have sent heavenwards has been answered. Is the christian god greater than the gods of the north?' He roared at the dark heavens.

He sought out a safe beach. When he saw one he ordered his men to row shorewards. They beached the ship and set

about mending the torn timbers. It took longer than they
expected and each minute which passed meant that Sigmund had less chance of catching up with Sixtus.

'It is only a patched job,' Sigmund said as he surveyed
the ship. The timber they had nailed to the side of the ship
looked like an ugly scar. 'We must move quickly now or
we will never catch them,' he told them. 'They cannot have
travelled far down the coast and we know that they can no
longer hide in the bays. Sigmund has flushed them out
into the open sea. It only remains to capture the treasure
and kill the monks. No one shall ever know what tricks
they have played on us.'

The crew members began to grumble amongst themselves. Instantly Sigmund had his dagger at the throat of
one of his men: 'The next man who grumbles dies.'

They pushed the great ship out into deep waters and
climbed aboard. They placed the oars in the oar ports and,
to the rhythm of drumbeats, began to row in pursuit of the
leather boat. For three hours they rowed, the sails helping
them forward. Rain came in windy squalls and cooled
their sweating bodies. As they passed Rubha a Mhail their
passage was noted. Immediately a rider set out across the
island, a journey of about twenty miles. He urged his
horse to the limits of its strength. Three hours later, Rolv
was told that Sigmund the Red, in pursuit of Sixtus, had
passed the northern tip of the island.

'How did Sigmund escape the dangerous rocks?' He
asked. No one could answer.

'Make ready to sail,' Rolv ordered his captains. 'We sail
all night, south–west. Keep within lantern distance of each
other. We will need the aid of oars. Change the oarsmen
every two hours. If the seas are clear, tomorrow we shall
meet Sigmund for the final encounter. By dawn we should
be in sight of Ireland.'

SIGMUND WISHED that he could stay the movement of the
sun. He needed two more hours of light. Darkness had

gathered in the east. There was still light in the western sky. The weather had cleared and as he looked at the large disk of sun on the horizon, he saw that it held a double sailed small boat.

'There they are!' He called to his crew, his long arm pointing. 'Directly west. We may catch them before dark,'

The oarsmen, tired after long hours of rowing, tried to gather strength within them. Sigmund beat heavily on the drum, roaring at them to keep in stroke: 'A final effort and we have them!'

Ahead, the leather boat made its way sluggishly west. Sixtus saw the Viking ship behind him. He looked at the sun. He wondered if he could keep ahead. Each time he looked at the Viking ship it was nearer and larger. He could make out the figure of Sigmund and hear the beating of the drum. He looked at the sun almost beneath the horizon, yet giving enough light to Sigmund. The huge ship would bear down on his frail boat.

And then, on the Viking ship, the oars broke rhythm and tangled. Sigmund had pushed his men too far. The ship turned in the water and the sails fell limp.

It gave Sixtus the time he needed. When Sigmund had reorganized his oarsmen and set his ship on course, darkness had fallen over the sea. 'They have escaped just when I had them in my grasp,' he cried.

Sixtus called to his monks to remain silent. There was little need for his order. They had watched in terror as the huge ship drew closer behind them.

Immediately darkness fell, Sixtus took the boat north. Later he turned west and finally he set his course for Ireland.

Sigmund sought the boat for an hour. Then he too set his course for Ireland. He could catch Sixtus in the morning dawn.

That night, the sea chase continued. The leather boat, with its great treasure, was pursued by the great Viking sea serpent under Sigmund which was pursued in turn by Rolv of Shetland's four ships. All sailed towards Ireland.

CHAPTER 11

The Final Combat

DAWN SPREAD ACROSS THE SEA. The tired monks looked anxiously towards the east where the light was grey. Sixtus listened to the sounds of the waves and the cry of the birds. They were nearing Ireland. He would beach the boat and they could take cover in the woods. As the light thickened and charged the waves with a dull pewter colour, he could smell the land.

'Shall we chant the matin prayers?' One of the monks enquired.

'Chant nothing, Brother. Do not even breathe. There will soon be quiet woods and lonely shores for chanting morning songs. Chant them in your hearts and pray for a good wind.'

'Are we out of danger, Sixtus?' Declan asked.

'No. Had the dawn been later then all would be well; but I fear the light.'

Now the sky was changing to silver, the bowl of light in the east growing larger. Ahead the monks could see the coast of Ireland.

'To the south is Ireland, Sixtus.' The monks called excitedly. 'We'll soon be safe.'

'And to the east lies danger, brothers,' he told them.

And then from the east, like a carrion bird, came the Viking ship. Sigmund the Red had finally tracked them down. Their journey had been futile. The monks stared in terror at the great ship they had avoided for so long.

'There will be an end to us. Sixtus took too many chances.

His sea sense betrayed him.'

Sixtus knew that time was against him. There was no trick he could now play upon the Viking.

'Diarmuid,' Declan called. 'Make your way down here.'

Diarmuid crawled over to where Declan sat at the bottom of the boat.

'I want you to bind the wound tightly so that the scar will not break.'

'You need rest.'

'Rest will come later. My strength has returned. Bind my scar with sailcloth and cut off the sleeves of my habit.'

Diarmuid took Declan's dagger and cut off the sleeves. Then he cut sail cloth into strips and bound them tightly about Declan's massive arm. As he looked up from his work of binding he could see Sigmund the Red standing on the prow of his ship, sword in hand.

'Look to the east, brothers' Enda said. 'More ships approach.' Far away and much smaller, they could make out four more Viking sails.

'Will you make the shore?' Declan asked Sixtus.

'Not now. We have not enough time left. The Viking ship approaches too swiftly.'

'Then I will board it and give you a final chance.'

'You endanger your life, Declan.'

'No, I protect the lives of others and I protect the great book. I will board the ship at the stern.'

'I will swing the boat about. Be ready to jump,' Sixtus said.

The Viking ship towered over the small boat as it bore down upon them. They looked at the figure of Sigmund the Red. Other than Declan, he was the largest man they had ever seen. With his horned helmet and red beard he was a ferocious figure.

'He wishes to cut us in two,' Sixtus called. 'Stand on the prow and make ready to jump.'

Just when it seemed certain that the base of the dragon headed prow would crash through their boat, Sixtus swung it sharply away. The Viking oars got caught in the small boat's masts. As the ship moved past the boat, Declan, on the fragile prow, threw himself forward and up, and clung to the side of the ship. He dragged himself on board and, standing on the stern, pulled his sword from its scabbard.

The Viking crewmen gazed at the massive figure above them with a two bladed sword in his hand. They knew it was the soldier monk and feared that he would run among them and slaughter them in their seats.

Meanwhile, Rolv's ships approached quickly. There was silence on the sea, silence in the ships. Sixtus, instead of racing to the shore and knowing that Rolv brought protection, hovered close by.

Sigmund the Red stood on the prow of his ship and looked with angry eyes at the monk. This man had brought ill luck to both himself and his ship. His enemies were gathering about him. Sigmund had the advantage in the fight. Declan's arm was bandaged and the ship rose and fell on a light wave.

Together both men roared out their battle cries and charged down the centre of the ship. They locked in combat. Their large swords clashed, sending off a shower of sparks. They pushed each other apart and charged again, hacking left and right.

'I call the fury of the gods upon you, monk, for having destroyed my ship. Your blood only can wash away my ill luck.'

They fought for a long time. The light now filled the summer sky. The breeze was soft and warm. Sigmund the Red knew that this might be his last battle. Strength surged like waves through him, strength which he thought he never possessed. His body was wet with sweat. He must wear the monk down, hope that his wound would begin to bleed. He looked at the bandage on his arm. It was stained red. He could now play him out.

Declan read his thoughts. He would have to make a quick end to the fight. His great strength was giving out.

Single combat: the soldier monk and the Viking leader

He could not move freely in the ship. His head was beginning to swim.

And then the sword was knocked from his hand. It slid across the timbers. Sigmund was bearing down upon him. He watched Sigmund's sword descend. Then, from somewhere within, his strength returned. Deftly he dodged the rough swing and, as the blade flashed down past him, he rushed forward and grabbed up his sword.

With a final burst of energy, he attacked Sigmund, his sword swinging in circles as it had done in former battle days. Sigmund listened to the sword music about him, stunned as Declan swept the sword from his grasp. It curved out over the sea and fell into the water.

'Put an end to him,' the Vikings roared from Rolv's ships. 'Rid the sea of the wolf.'

Sigmund waited for the blow to descend. It did not. Declan looked at the sword, with which he had fought so many battles and reaching his arm back, threw it high over the Viking ships. It spun as it rose in a bright arc. It caught the sun and sent off a thousand silver flashes. Then it fell into the sea.

'I am finished with blood and battles,' he said. 'I will seek out some monastery where I can be alone, where I can have ease of mind and pray for those I killed.'

'Why did you not kill me?' Sigmund roared in Norse but Declan did not understand. As he turned away, Sigmund pulled out his dagger to plunge it in his broad back. The blow never struck Declan. Rolv had noticed the move. He drew his dagger and flung it at Sigmund. It caught him in the heart. He stood for a moment, his mouth open and his eyes staring. Then he fell forwards, dead. The flight and the pursuit were over.

'Never have I seen such a great sailor and such a great warrior,' Rolv said much later as he prepared to leave with his ships. 'Go now to some inland monastery and finish your great book in quiet surrounds. I will tell the monks at Iona that the great book is safe.'

'Go in peace, Rolv,' Sixtus said.

And having given the Viking a blessing, he directed two of the monks to row shorewards. When they reached the beach Brother Paul knelt and kissed the sand of Ireland. The great book, upon which he had laboured for so long, had been carried safely across the sea.

Somewhere inland, surrounded by birdsong and beside a quiet stream they would finish the book. Somewhere off the western coast lay a stony island wind swept and desolate, where Declan would build a beehive hut and live out his days praying for all soldiers who die in battle.